Brenda

A Whimsical Look at a Fallen Star

Gerald Burke Leonard

Hollywood Beach Publishing, LLC

For information address
Hollywood Beach Publishing Company, Inc.
3225 South Harbor Boulevard,
Channel Islands Harbor, CA 93035

Published by Hollywood Beach Publishing Company, Inc.

Library of Congress Catalog
LCCN 2013906395

ISBN 978-0-9891902-0-6

First published in the United States by HBP. LLC. 2013

Dedicated to

Brenda

Actually, for all those Brenda's
– by whatever name –
in Hollywood and beyond, trapped by the
delusion of grandeur created by
their own beauty
and fed upon by man's avarice.

The Opening Salvo

"Life can be hard. Just ask someone who has no money. While often inarticulate, such people can remonstrate the pitfalls of the economy, the inadequacies of presidential domestic policy and a litany of injustices befallen them because of the poverty they face. Such individuals are closer to reality than those of us insulated by possessions and frivolities mistaken for necessities. Life is even harder for those for whom money and possessions had been an integral part of their lives but for whom such vanities and comforts are only a fleeting memory. Ask Brenda. She knows.

So who is Brenda that she should be quoted as to the economy and the value of money before citing Chairman Greenspan, the sage of the Federal Reserve system?

It's nice of you to ask. Brenda could use your understanding and probably a few bucks as well."

"Why are you talking about me this way and why the hell are you using that little tape recorder?" asked Brenda.

"It's quite simple, Brenda... well maybe not so simple really. Let me try to explain," stated the tweed-covered academic slowly sucking a cherry aroma from the Dunhill Red Bark pipe clenched tightly between teeth that had mellowed. The professor-interviewer was the quintessential oxymoron. All the trappings of a university professor could not conceal his basic insecurities and inabilities to function within a societal context. His suit hung, draped over his narrow shoulders like so much wilted lettuce hanging from the edge of a salad plate. His glasses bore a striking resemblance to upturned Coke bottles; his tie, a clip-on, and his J.C. Penney's wash-and-wear shirt lacked the crispness of a self-assured professional. His shirt bore more creases than the bottom of a fat baby or the face of an aging movie star.

The two sat tenuously on an MTA bus stop bench on Hollywood Boulevard. The professor had found the subject for his research thesis in the Hollywood Reporter, one of those T&A rags in the ever-present vendor boxes that populate all the principal thoroughfares of Hollywood and the Valley. Their pervasiveness was akin to the number of aging, balding men who would gather along the Boulevard to watch trendy young girls flaunt body parts that could only be imagined in the Midwest but were part of the everyday landscape of Southern California.

Between black-belching buses, the throttled thunder of Hell's Angels devotees showing their impatience for traffic signals, and the twitching nervousness of the one-time porn industry celeb, the professor attempted to learn about the social stigmatization of the porn industry on those "retired" from its clutches.

Brenda.... A Whimsical Look at a Fallen Star

The painfully unique social combination sat rigidly facing each other as if braced for confrontation. The professor sat hunched over, his rounded shoulders demonstrating a minimal level of testosterone present in his frail and beleaguered physique. Brenda sat one cheek only on the graffiti-encrusted bench her head swiveling continuously. Was she looking for a score, a "Hollywood" producer, some muscle-laden sub-intellect who could light up her fancy or was she just nervous. . . the jury was out on the question and the professor struggled to interrupt her interruptions and gain her attention for a spate of time. The midday sun slapped down heavily on the two individuals who could have been from different planets. The blistering heat enlivened the color of Brenda's cavernous cleavage creating a tenderness that she stroked for comfort. The professor's eyes lost focus and drool spilled from the corner of his lips; his ability to rise from the bus bench would render him a social enigma. He knew he must be rigid, so to speak, and focus on the questions he had so thoughtfully enumerated as the foundation for his research grant.

"You see Brenda, that fifty dollars I gave you... it wasn't for your services. Oh no. I'm not interested in that. No not at all. I simply want to talk." The interviewer's eyebrows arched upward in an expression of hope and clarity as he managed to extricate Brenda attention from a young stud whose pants were so tight one could make out the president's face on the quarter in his pocket.

"What do you mean? Are you some kind of freak or somethin'?" Who pays for it," the words barked from her ruby red lips "and doesn't take it? Some kind of freakin' pervert you are. I'm getting the hell out of here."

"Wait! Please. I don't mean to offend you."

3

"I'm not offended you asshole. It takes more than you've got to get to me. I just don't trust you. Look at you! You come down here to my neighborhood dressed up like it was a Sunday social or you're getting married. You pay me fifty bucks and tell me you want to talk. That's just not right and people like you can't be trusted." The cacophony that was the business of the boulevard suitably covered the tone of the rant.

The interviewer tried to break into the woman's tirade as his horn-rimmed spectacles slid from the bridge of his nose clattering to the concrete. "Wait, you don't understand," he pleaded.

Brenda abruptly interrupted the professor, "I saw someone on the TV say Jeffrey Daumer was a nice guy to talk to... till he ate those kids. No mister... you get the hell away from me and leave me alone." She concluded her remarks with a dazzling display of spittle that spewed as if to emphasize her contempt as her breasts heaved about like two old walruses in mating season. Her public display that would have called for incarceration or institutionalization in many states was barely a recognizable event in Hollywood. Throngs of tourists, junkies, and retired old people who had gotten trapped in the clutches of the degenerative process that was the loss of the glitter of Hollywood passed by mumbling to themselves looking for respite from the sun's blinding rays.

In the heyday of Hollywood every manner of young man and young woman flocked to the glitz and glamour of "the boulevard." Like Lana Turner they would be discovered and there would be instant fame and fortune. The reality of not being discovered was a slow and painful process for many who hung on to the dream even after their looks had deteriorated and their income and earning potential dwindled to nothing. Now they were stuck in a seven hundred square

foot stucco construct that sat sandwiched between two parking lots, a bank tower and a Pussycat Theater – or some other harbinger of the new reality of Hollywood.

"Wait. Can I give you more money? Here's another twenty. Just calm down I just want to talk to you," the professor said apprehensively as he clutched a crumpled bill with bony, little white fingers.

Brenda was already on her feet which rode high above the sidewalk on her WalMart-purchased platform heels. Brenda's outfit, costume to some, was an uncoordinated combination of stripes and patterns in a myriad of colors and fabric finishes. Her skirt was too short to permit her to bend over and pick up a one hundred dollar bill that might someday be found on the sidewalk. A popular Chicago disc jockey had once characterized this type of skirt when he said on the air, "if skirts get any shorter girls will have more cheeks to powder and more hair to comb." The highly popular "rock jock" was summarily fired immediately after his clever twist of the tongue.

Turning her back to the befuddled professor, she quickly bent from the waste to grab her oversized purse from the end of the bus bench and proved the rock jock to be the sage of the times. Her spandex micro-mini rode its way up her supple legs as she bent revealing spider veins coursing their way the length of her muscled thighs and peaking over the tops of the garter-held nylons. Her stretching also became a revelation in the fine art of body tattooing with a likeness of a cherry perched in a precipitous location on her backside and just below the tautly-drawn thong or G-string that dove down into undefined darkness. The interviewer realized in that brief observation he wasn't certain what he was seeing; he just wished that he hadn't seen it – at least not up so close.

Her things in tow, Brenda mingled her way into the phalanx of pedestrian traffic with a command of her presence like George Patton on his move through Europe. Her more-than-ample breasts were stuffed into a grossly-undersized bra which combined with a dramatically revealing scooped neck tank top caused Brenda to jiggle and bounce her way leaving the stunned professor in her wake. The professor's pipe dangled precariously from his lower lip spilling its reddened contents onto his lap as he took in the professional strut that had gained Brenda her fame.

Teasingly turning her head in reverse she offered a parting thought for the professor: "I was a star, a movie star. And you ARE an asshole."

The Professor

The pipe ashes seared a patch through the fibrous cloth after the interviewer's pipe fell from his mouth. A look of shock wiped over his face like a splash of aftershave following a dull blade. Professor Malcom Hughes, Rhodes Scholar, and Chairman of the USC Psychology Department couldn't put together a coherent thought. Hughes was mentally adrift at being able to explain the manner in which he had just been put in his place by someone so many levels beneath him on the social scale that dominated his motivations. After all, he was a tenured scholar at one of our nation's most prestigious academic institutions. When he spoke, as with Smith Barney, people listened . . . at least as Hughes believed it to be. Not Brenda, however. She had a mind of her own and a body that belonged to the thousands who had rented it over the course of her "professional" career.

Jumping, Hughes was finally stirred to action by the singeing that burned into his manhood, such as it was, from the smoldering ashes. If Brenda had known she had gotten the professor hot down there she would have floated down Hollywood Boulevard on her WalMart platform heels with a smerk rather than a look of contempt. Hughes sprang from the bus bench screaming profanities, kicked over his brief case and nearly fell head-first into a trash container – it too leaving not a square inch without the symbols of the Latino gangs who saw Hollywood as their "hood." Hughes pulled a 12-ounce bottle of Sparkletts' from his tattered case and freely poured its contents directly onto his damaged area – a small geyser of steam rising from his testicles. "Oh Jesus, oh Jesus they burn. Goddamn that arrogant bitch. She can't do this to me. Oh Jesus they burn. And now all these freaks on the Boulevard are going to see me, them, before I can get back to the room," hissed the balding and gaunt specimen of the "before" pictures for body building ads.

After running frantically back to the Holiday Inn just off the Boulevard at Highland where he had rented a room as a field headquarters for his research, Hughes finally found some relief from the first degree burns he managed to self-inflict by imposing himself into the sink and blasting the icy water onto himself.

As Hughes stood in front of the full-length mirror just inside Holiday Inn room 212, his pants and shorts caught around his knees and his damaged goods in his left hand, he picked around at the soreness with his right. An abrupt knock at the door was followed by an immediate entry by a striped-clad service worker from some Central American country. In less than one second, the maid took in the horror (or is it whore) show taking place in front of the mirror and crashed her way back through the door as fast as she had come in. As Hughes forgot his pain and pulled his pants to full staff, so to

speak, he peered out the door to see a waddling middle-aged Latina running pall mall down the hallway screaming in some unintelligible language that only she and God might understand.

"Ahhhhh! What the hell is happening?"

"I'm a professional. I can deal with this. Two crazy women in a row.. . . that's not a common day for me but that's women for you. It's unfortunate they can't be the rational, logical people that men are... well, at least educated men. . . highly educated, men. Now. First things first and all will be back in logical order in no time."

By his accounts, Hughes was a fastidious dresser – neat, orderly, never an undone tie (but then, clip-ons can't dangle loosely) his vest buttoned properly, a shine on his penny loafers and all the other accoutrements of an establishment type from that time in our society when anti-establishment was the rage.

"Okay, first things first. I'll call the office and have Dennis bring over a spare pair of pants from my office closet. That will do to get me out of this hell hole and back where I belong."

"Hello, Dennis... this is Doctor Hughes. I' like you to...."

Thirty minutes later Dennis is standing in Hughes' post-renovation hotel room staring at the quandary before him. Hughes began the process of stripping away the damaged pants in preparation for donning the wrinkled khakis that Dennis brought. The hot ashes had burned right through the front of Hughes' J.C. Penney's white briefs, the kind he had worn since childhood. The unfortunate location of the burned

material left Hughes dangling in plain sight. Dennis's eyes were pulled as if by magnetism to a fixed stare on a sight he wished he had never seen and which would recur in his dreams nightmarishly for years to come.

Without warning the room door was crashed upon from the hallway, bursting open. Stepping in behind a drawn automatic handgun was the next level of escalation to Hughes' unraveling drama. First in, behind the gun, was a swarthy replica of a post-career Marlon Brando accompanied by the blushing, rotund Latina maid and a third measure of security, a Hulk Hogan look-a-like dressed in a two-tone blue security guard uniform.

Just when the impeccable Dr. Malcolm Hughes thought he had solved the debacle in which he found himself, there were three new witnesses to an apparent professor-assistant affair that was being played out in Room 212 like the Mad Hatter's tea party. "Oh my God." The words dribbled out of his mouth like so much spinach on the face of a two year old. He now had to explain the attention that Dennis was demonstrating as lasciviousness to the intruders but which was actually a sense of shock and awe on the part of the impressionable young man.

"Damn that Brenda. This is all her fault."

Enter the "Gestapo"

The air was electric with tension as the young graduate assistant argued his case before the epitome of eccentricity. His arms flailing about like twin windmills in a gale, Dennis launched into the discord that Professor Hughes' had created as a consequence of the conundrum initiated by Brenda. "I don't see, Professor Hughes, how my being gay added to your problems before the University Ethics Committee. I did nothing other than bring your pants as I was told. The goons broke in and then my next job was getting bail money. So what did I do wrong?"

"I've calmed down, Dennis, so maybe I can explain to you what perception is all about. You fucking twit."

Hughes uncharacteristically jerked at his shirt collar to loosen its incapacitating effects on his ability to deal with the "C-"student. Tossing two non-prescription tablets into his mouth he reached for his ever-present Sparkletts bottled water as he continued to lecture Dennis on the fine points of human intercourse, or human interaction, as he corrected himself with

the student assistant. The level of distraction continued to exceed his ability to function and he next bumped a cup of three-day old coffee that spilled onto the paper he had just produced for the American Academy of Psychologists' annual meeting. "Shit, fire! What next? Out! Please just leave Dennis. We will talk later. There are simply too many distractions right now."

"Whatever you say Mein Herr," Dennis rebuffed as he sashayed flippantly from his mentor's office.

Turning from his stare at Dennis's exaggerated movements used to accentuate his male-to-male calling card, Professor Hughes turned back to his attempt to dry the coffee stains from the object of his pride, *The Psychological Effects of Male Enhancement Drugs on the Ego of Aging American Males*. "Dennis, Brenda... what in the hell is this world coming to? Why can't they simply be like me?" he spoke as if to someone but only to the vacuous confines of his cluttered office. After tidying up as best possible Hughes, paused for a quick mental check with reality. *Was he still the talented professor of psychology at one of the premier universities in America? Yes! Okay, then all is going to be fine. . . just a series of unfortunate, unlikely circumstances occurring simultaneously within one physical point in the universe. That's normal, isn't it?*

"Normal. Yes, normal. Role model in fact." His self-assurance in his intellectual superiority returning, Hughes began to strut about his office toward the window to observe those lesser human beings who had not, nor would ever hope to achieve, his level of intellectualism, and superiority by extension. A throat-clearing at his doorway abruptly interrupted his reverie; he pirouetted as if on cue by the dance instructor to see the head of the Ethics Committee standing with his arms crossed over his chest, peering over the tops of

his half glasses. The room darkened as he spoke; only the light of hell's fire and brimstone shone forth with the over-pronunciation of each "H" in his rhetorical diatribe. "Normal? he asks. You're describing yourself, Dr. Hughes? In what lifetime would you have been found normal?" Dr. Steingrit, the University Chancellor's equivalent of the Internal Affairs Division of the police department, the Inquisition's lead tormentor, or even the head of the Gestapo in Hitler's merry band of fanatics was poised to deliver Hughes back to whatever planet that he called home. "We have to talk Hughes."

"Fine come in, please have a seat," Hughes gestured to a chair piled with sundry papers, an umbrella without a handle, and a scattered pile of essay exams all of which seem to be marked in seventy-two point type with a bright red "F."

"No. Thank you anyway. I'm sure that your office is more hospitable than it looks." Steingrit's eyes wandered about the clutter and wondered to what degree what he saw reflected the condition of Hughes' mind and perhaps the problems that had brought him to Hughes' office. "No. What I had in mind is you sitting once again before the Review Panel on Monday morning, next. We will have our final recommendations at that time as to the possible revocation of your tenure or whatever other outcome we collectively decide upon."

"You can't revoke my tenure," Hughes choked out in a part shriek, part plea, and a part of something else that caused the befuddled self-styled academic to choke on his own spittle.

"Actually, Hughes, you have brought incredible embarrassment upon your department and the university as a whole. It is not the sort of thing that we promote nor can we

even tolerate. You have a week to put together your oral defense of the circumstances surrounding this little debacle in the unlikely hope that it will sway enough of the members to move in your direction.

"I never...." sputtered an exasperated Chairman of the Psychology Department.

"Actually, it appeared that you did and there is a police file to so attest." The portly modern day SS officer seemed to click his heels together as he turned to leave. As he left the doorway Hughes abstractly became aware how much lighter his office seemed when the portly, bushy eye browed agent of the Chancellor wasn't blocking all the light coming in from the hallway.

Hmmmmm. What in the hell am I going to do to get these paper-chasing fanatics off my back and let me get back to work? I have my AAP paper to re-do, thanks to the coffee. And I have the research to consider maintaining my grant from the U.S. Department of Education. That means Brenda. Oh Christ, Brenda. That is how all this got started. Brenda! How to deal with Brenda. . . . His thoughts were starting to crystallize as he paced about the crowded, cluttered space, hands clasped behind his back. The replacement three-piece tweed suit had performed admirably to overheat the man whose internal thermometer was probably throbbing at about one hundred forty degrees, his grayed shirt now transparent with befouled perspiration drenching it, among the myriad signs of a tempestuous storm that was rising both within his bowels and in his "superior" mind. "Ohhhh, shiiiiit – the only words that overarched his growling stomach.

Brenda's Analysis

Tapping her two-tone nails against the Formica table top with an increasingly severe touch, Brenda ripped into a tirade against the weird little university professor. "The more I think about it Debbie, the sillier it becomes. How many tricks have you faced that say they just want to talk? Do you know how pissed this little dink of a man made me... how can any man pass up all of this and just want to talk?" Brenda's eyes did a quick scan of her voluptuous proportions, still tight where tight was critical, still soft where it was important. She wafted her hand in a gesture to bring her best friend's attention to focus.

"I don't know Brenda, it seems pretty weird to me," replied Brenda's neighbor.

Sitting there on the 1950's blonde wood couch, on either side of the protruding spring, the two began to laugh until rivulets of tears began to cut courses through the overly laden rouge that caked Debbie's face. Coal black streamers of mascara trickled down through the bright red circles of rouge and formed a surrealistic image that was the former hooker's

face. For her part Brenda never noticed the freakish appearance of her friend even though her own appearance would draw stares anywhere beyond her beloved Hollywood Boulevard domain.

"So what are you going to do?" asked the woman who wore a painter's pallet for a face.

"About what?" challenged Brenda as if there had been no prior dialogue.

They looked at each other and spontaneously burst into another round of laughter.

"Oh... you mean about that goofy-looking little man from yesterday."

"Yeah, him."

"I wasn't going to do anything. Why?"

"Well... money's money, isn't it?" asked the painted lady.

Brenda sat there for a moment, rubbing the laughter tears from her eyes. Then, standing before her friend, feet apart, she thrust out her chemically-endowed chest spontaneously popping a button like a missile across the couch and said, "yeah, when you've got 'em, use 'em and to their best advantage. Right?"

"Right!" chimed in her awe struck friend.

"Okay then... we need a plan of action. Just like in the movies," stated the former porn queen.

"You mean just like in the movies you made, Brenda?" asked Debbie.

16

"No, sweet love. Those movies had no plan of action. Hell, most didn't even have dialogue."

The two looked at each other and began a new round of laughter that consumed them to the point of Brenda falling doubled-up onto the couch and hugging her good friend.

"No, Debbie, what I meant to say is, let's figure out how we can milk this dweeb for as much as possible. And the best part is I'll never let him have any of my goodness."

"You'll save it for someone special, right, Brenda?" Debbie asked in a tone of sincerity.

"No, I don't think I have much left to save Deb and there never was a man that special anyway. No, what I've got in mind is giving this guy his earful in a way that just pulls him along further and further down the road of wanton abandon taking him right to the edge of the cliff."

"I see. Then when you get him there he'll want more and end up falling off that cliff. Right."

"Nope, I thought at that point I'd push the sucker off and maybe throw a rock after him."

The two held a serious stare into each other's eyes for a moment and then the two erupted into still another round of laughter that once again consumed them.

"It's time for a beer and then we can go strut all this good stuff on the Boulevard for a while for old time's sake. What do you say Deb?"

"Let's do it."

Money is Money

"Professor Hughes. I found out who you are through Arnie, the desk clerk at the Hollywood Holiday Inn. It seems there is still some value in a freebie from time to time, besides, Arnie always saw to it I had clean sheets and a working TV in the rooms I got."

"How very nice for you Brenda. . . . After the little nightmare that began unraveling when you stormed from the bus bench last week. I have to ask: what brings you here?" asked a troubled Professor Hughes, a quizzical look squirreled onto his gaunt face dominated by a proboscis the envy of any walrus and ears borrowed from Dumbo.

Brenda was not known for her fastidious sense of fashion or conventional use of makeup -- the concept of style was beyond her comprehension. Her presence on the campus of the University of Spoiled Children, as USC is commonly

known in Los Angeles, drew more odd looks than a Notre Dame victory over the Trojans.

Bothered? Out of place? Self-conscious? Not Brenda. She owned the world and these rich kids could look all they wanted. It would be an education for them... a chance to see a film queen. Her smirk was not subtle as she walked past Tommy Trojan. The expression might have even been haughtiness. Rumor had it that even Tommy's bronze-encrusted features turned slightly to follow the strut in the short shorts.

Haughtiness was not quite what spilled over the face of the professor who stood to be censured for his involvement in a series of questionable acts that were in one way or another tied to this woman. In fact, the expression on Professor Hughes face was one of sheer terror.

"I thought I should try to mend the fences professor doctor. It's been more than a week since we spoke and I feel badly that we didn't get off on the right foot the other day. I thought, well what the hell, if he wants to talk, okay I'll talk," Brenda said with certain dramatic appeal – a condition that was never required of her in her movie career. "You seem really tense doctor professor. Think it might loosen you up a little if I gave you a uh, you know...."

"First of all, it is Professor Hughes or Doctor Hughes. Not professor doctor or doctor professor. Second of all, no. There will be no illicit activity here in my office."

"Oh then, shall we head for my place above the Ding Vinh Vietnamese Liquor Store on Ivar Street? She asked as she started to rise from her chair.

Hughes began to pace thoughtfully trying to decide how to unload this social aberration. His quandary, however, was that she was the key object of his investigation for his DOE grant – the source of his added income beyond his teaching stipend. Yet, if Dr. Steingrit happened by there would be no review panel – period! Steingrit would surely chase him from the campus with a field hockey stick or have the interior linemen from the football team, those nameless hunks of humanity who seemed to be all bulk and no brain, crush him into a dumpster behind Clavell Hall. Hell, he thought, it was bad enough for his image that anyone saw this side show attraction from a Midwest county fair sitting in his office. None of the respectable little sexpots from the San Fernando Valley would bother to even pretend they found him cute as the means to maintain their grade in his class – without even attending. *No*, he thought, *this is as close to a lose-lose scenario as he had ever encountered. Kind of like the President getting the country embroiled in a meaningless war so as to distract the American public from his failing domestic policies.*

"I tell you Brenda. I very much would like to get together with you but my schedule right now is a little frightful. Perhaps we can schedule another time... another place. Would that be acceptable to you?"

"Of course, love, whatever makes you happy. You will be paying me for my time as we had originally discussed."

"Yes, of course, a deal is a deal."

"Good, then I need thirty bucks for a cab to get back to Hollywood."

"Yes, of course you do. And I need some Excedrin, several." Trying to regain control, he offered, "I'll call you to set something up."

As she adjusted one of the overweight "twins" huddled in her tank top, Brenda was quick to retort. "No. I'll call you. I have to use the phone at the Chevron or in the lobby of the Pussycat Theater. I'll call you." Command and control re-established, Brenda swung about on her platforms and began a sequence of moves drawn straight from one of her movies.

Operation Gouge

The temperature was seventy-five at Venice Beach, eighty-five in downtown Los Angeles, one hundred and three in the San Fernando Valley, and one hundred fourteen stifling degrees in Cucamonga – wherever that is. The sun was out, if only theoretically, since in Los Angeles it is seldom seen. This was the kind of spring day that had *beach* written all over it. The campus air conditioning systems were on the fritz, it was the dead week before finals and little was stirring.

Professor Hughes sat in his office pretending to emote an aura of professionalism that is required of academics. He had eked his way through the review panel that wanted desperately to send the geeky, pseudo-academic nerd off the campus forever if not directly to hell. Hughes's primary argument had been centered on the contributory value his survey research regarding Brenda held. After all there were so many young women in the Los Angeles area who had been sucked into the black hole of social existence by the pornographic industry; his research would offer a foothold for such young women to reclaim their tattered lives.

Unknown to the balance of the review committee, was the tawdry affair being played out by Dr. Steingrit – the guardian of virtue on the campus. Steingrit, for his part, had been assuaged by the knowledge that Hughes had used his Minox to snap any number of pictures of he and professor Helen Brighthurst, Ph.D., visiting professor from Indiana University sex research clinic. – in the most compromising of positions. Steingrit had been checked. . . temporarily, but he had not been checkmated.

Hughes had caught the ever-horny couple in a mutual grope on more than one occasion, hiding in a janitor's closet, behind the bookshelves in Steingrit's office and even behind the bleachers at the university's track stadium. They acted like two rabbits in heat looking for a spot to bring their lurid affair to culmination.

The air conditioning belched out a refusal to work overtime in the extremes of the southern California heat wave that rendered the Psychology Department just a few Fahrenheit's above the campus incinerator, or so it seemed to those caught in the clutches of the brick infernos whose windows were sealed shut.

As he sat at his desk, salty beads of sweat sliding south from his arm pits, his shoes kicked off but his suit jacket still buttoned religiously, Hughes' mind was caught on a point of intellectual curiosity - the moral, social, and political dilemma relating to the prospect of enforced birth control for people below some intellectual threshold. As his mind configured the methods of enforcement his face unwittingly contorted into a gleeful composition that could not have been more than skin deep. His mind was enjoying the thought of such control. He, of course, would be appointed as the procurator of the process. Women would be coming to him begging for permission to have his baby and it would be his

sole province to set any dispensations to the ruling. What would be his price he wondered? Should he charge a fee? Should he, perhaps, be the only individual permitted to impregnate such women who begged for the right? Such intellectual curiosity was the stuff of an advanced philosophical pursuit. He knew it and he likewise knew that the others about him on the campus had no capacity to comprehend the value and meaning of such thought.

Riiiing! Riiiiing! The shrill sound of the antiquated phone system jolted Hughes from his point of intellectual drama. His swivel rocker tipped backward throwing his legs upward as if he were practicing for the USC diving team and the non-descript clutch of papers that he held shot into the air above his desk as if propelled by a cannon. As the papers wafted to the ground like windless kites one settled atop the phone entitled "The Effects of Birth Control on the Minority Population." As he reached for the phone Hughes brushed the paper aside and made a mental note that he would have to continue the daydream he had been having. It seemed quite satisfying.

"Hello. Yes, what is it," said an irritated Hughes.

"It's Brenda Doctor Professor Hughes. Did you want to start the talking today? You know, the social intercourse." Brenda giggled as she asked an exasperated Hughes about beginning the interview process.

"I'm not fully prepared yet. But I supposed we could get started. At a minimum it would get me out of this cracker box of an office."

"Back to the Holiday Inn again or the bus bench and all the distractions of the Boulevard?" Brenda intoned as Hughes contemplated his more strategic option.

"No. I think not. Let me think about that one a moment." Hughes, normally clad in one of his ubiquitous gabardine J.C. Penny suits as a trade-off to his tweed options thought about the heat; he thought about having to interview the walking commercial for rouge; and he thought about his commitment to avoid being seen with Brenda by the female population of the USC campus.

"I have it! Let's conduct our little discussion at the beach."

"Great! I can wear my new thong bikini," Brenda sounded thrilled at the prospect of being able to remind people of her once proud assets. In a voice of sheer glee, Brenda blurted, "which beach, Professor Doctor?" She stood at the phone booth at the Chevron on Sunset Boulevard as the geeky professor seemed to play directly into her hands. Her excitement boundless at this point, Brenda began to spring up and down making conversation on the phone somewhat truncated. As she sprung up and down the twins elected to bounce on their own and at a different pace trying their damndest to set themselves free.

"Brenda, I told you to not... oh never mind." Hughes paused to consider the most likely beach to be able to observe the best looking girls wearing the absolute least. "How about Manhattan Beach, Brenda?"

"I can't get there. Let's do Venice Beach." The giggling began anew.

"Oh what the hell, I suppose that's fine," he conceded.

"Besides, Maury, is there. He's a weight lifter you know. He was in serious competition a few years back. He

also carried me into a few motel rooms. What a gentleman."
Her voice tailed off as if she were heading back a few years on
a solo trip.

"I want to see Maury, Professor Doctor. Let's meet
at Venice. Or would you prefer to come by and pick me up?"

One of the quickest responses ever out of Hughes
mouth followed Brenda's question.

"No. No I don't think that would be possible Brenda.
My car's a wreck; you wouldn't like it. It's all cluttered with
things… papers, books… you know."

"I'd believe that if you told me it was cluttered with
men's magazines."

"You've seen my car?" asked an astonished Hughes.

Darting back to her flat above the Vietnamese liquor
store, pulling together an ensemble for the beach took precious
little effort. Brenda's entire beach outfit was compressed
within a single clenched fist as she danced around the one-
room reminder of a 1950s studio set.

If You Don't Succeed . . .

"Ooh, it tickles," giggling and jiggling, a jubilant Brenda blurted. "Don't you just love the sensation?"

"Huh?" Professor Hughes' level of distraction was akin to a high school cheerleader's involvement in geometry class. Never had he seen so many *things* to gawk at all in one place – as if they had been placed there for his personal gratification. The challenge had become how to keep from running into something while he walked and stared. The drooling. . . well, that was an unintended consequence that had wetted the cuff of his coat sleeve. Hughes' predicament was much like the old conundrum of rubbing one's forehead and patting the stomach at the same time. Hughes wasn't really up to the task.

"What'd you say?"

"I said, Mr. Eyes-Everywhere, don't you love the feeling?"

"What feeling?"

"Sitting here in the sand in my thong with all this tanning lotion on the sand stuck to me in places is hard to clean away. You know where, don't you Mr. Eyes-Everywhere? I saw you staring at my behind when I bent over."

"Good God Brenda, you bent at the waist with that string thong on and your ass was two inches from my face. What's not to see?' retorted the lobster-colored professor.

"I know you were looking. You wanted to see what you're not going to get."

"Oh Christ, Brenda, could we get back to the task at hand. We're at your favorite beach, I am burning like a marshmallow dropped into the campfire, and we have never managed to get to the point yet." An exasperated Hughes rotated his head nearly one hundred eighty degree to watch a nineteen year old strut past spilling from her postage stamp-size bikini.

"Yes, I see what you mean" shot Brenda in response. "We're having a hard time, no pun intended, I'm sure. You seem to be very up for all work and no play... or do I have that just reversed?"

"I need to get out of this infernal sun – I'm dying. Furthermore, the sun is too bright to read my notes and questions."

"Over by the weightlifter's area there is a small café. I'm sure there is a place for people like you." Brenda's eyes rolled around in sheer disbelief of her own words.

"And what did you mean by that?" challenged the two-legged lobster whose scrawny, hairy legs were as bright a color as the crown of his head. "Damn, we were only sitting there for a few minutes, I swear."

"What did I mean? I was referring to people like you who are follicly-challenged... you know... that glow that you have where you might otherwise have hair, the chrome dome. We need to get you into the shade before your head blisters and before your vision is impaired. God knows, you'd have no sex life at all if your eyes stopped working. Right Professor Doctor?"

"Okay. I accept your tangential reference to my unwitting sense of distractibility. The café there would be fine, thank you."

Two beers and a plateful of fries later Brenda consented to begin the interview session by reminding the doctor that the hour is wearing on and that they probably had better begin to think in terms of making their way back across to Hollywood.

A disgruntled Hughes grabbed Brenda by the wrists and spoke very slowly, adroitly and directly into her masticating face. "Listen to me. I have to conduct a series of interviews with you. It is the foundation for a research project that I have contracted to do with the U.S. Department of Education. My continued employment at the university rests largely on my successful publication of the findings of this set of interviews. There was a big deal made out of the value of this research following the Heidi Fleiss notoriety about prostitution in Los Angeles. I must ask you a bunch of questions and probe deeply into your background, you know, why you've pursued the lifestyle that you have and all that. Now, are we clear on this?"

"Sure doc." The sound of French fries being masticated garbled her few words as they worked their way through a mush of potatoes crammed into her gob. "But would you mind letting go? I have to eat these quickly – their getting cold."

The professor let loose his grip which had become increasingly menacing as his mind became more absorbed in his self-importance and that of his research. "Sorry."

"Shoot. How long is this going to take because I want to get back to the *Palace on Ivar*. That's my digs, you know, where I live."

"The Palace on Ivar?"

"Well, that just a nickname. You should have seen the shit hole I lived in before."

"This is going to take multiple sessions Brenda. I'm going to give you a homework assignment. I want you to break up your life into a series of events that led you to becoming a whore."

There was a long pause before the next word was spoken. A dark cloud had seemed to settle directly over their little café table and a storm was looming. It may have been a psycho-social drama or it may have been forecast on the Channel 7 weather the night before. Regardless, it brought a solemnity that crushed the effervescence of the bubbly, jiggly ex-porno queen.

"You know. No one ever called me that before and never . . . never once did I think of myself as a whore. Thank you doc."

The "Bull-Dyke" from Wellesley

Hughes managed to resurrect the interview process within the limited time before Brenda demanded to catch the route 426 bus back to Hollywood; however, it went dismally. Confrontational, anti-intellectual, and tense would characterize the atmosphere created by the conversation often punctuated with outright bursts of hostility and barbs from both sides. The bubbly princess of porn who managed to get from one day to the next, somehow, now had been labeled a whore. It cut deeply. The only salve she could work into the wound was the belief that Hughes's only sexual gratification most likely came from making such perverse statements to women.

Brenda slid the micro mini up over her sand-encrusted legs, lathered in oils and creams and sanded by her two hours on the Venice beach. She had vented and steamed her disapproval at Hughes's lack of gentility and the inappropriate moniker: whore. More than angered, she was wounded and took her limited pride with her as she tramped past the bubble-eyed tourists to the bus stop.

For his part, Hughes unabashedly splayed his vulgar appearance across a recliner, donned some shades and proceeded to ogle everyone – everyone female, every female between sixteen and thirty-five. Only those, however, who appeared to be over seventy-five looked back in his direction and then most likely to laugh at the charbroiled color of his skin. The excesses of his prurient interests were exceeded only by the deepening color of his burning flesh. He would pay later for his sexual focus. At this time, thoughts of his predicament flip-flopped through his sunbaked brain like the distracting sound of the rubber thongs worn by the teeny boppers who giggled and teased as they passed the human lobster.

When some muscle-laden weightlifter that looked like Conan the Barbarian stood casting a shadow over the barbecued Hughes, the latter's focus was interrupted: "Hey, dude, you look like I could shove a skewer up your ass, throw on some sauce and serve you for dinner." *Time to leave,* Hughes thought. It would be a difficult trip home and a very difficult night; his pending investment in aloe would mean not eating for a week.

Sitting at his office in anticipation of the next interview, Hughes realized he had blundered when he had called Brenda a whore. *What the hell have I gotten myself into?* He thought. The rail of a man, clothed in his three-piece tweed suit, the summer heat notwithstanding, vexed over the dilemma in which he now found himself. He had contracted with the DOE people in Washington to complete this study and had taken a large advance on the project. He had to produce results and he knew full well that that plump, over-ripe melon of a woman at DOE to whom he had to report was counting on his failure. She had wanted some dyke of a professor of Women's Studies from Wellesley to do the work but he had underbid Wellesley and the woman who, he

thought laughingly, had more of a moustache than he. The federal procurement process being what it was, he was taken based on the low bid regardless of how the bureaucrats had finagled to twist the outcome against him in favor of his collegial adversary.

He would have to succeed even though he was programmed to fail and now the thought occurred to him that the woman with the hyphenated last name from Wellesley had probably gotten to Brenda to have her make his life a living hell. *No. That's not possible*, he concluded. However, his body language never demonstrated conviction.

Perhaps, Hughes thought speaking to himself, *I could change the principal subject of the investigation and get someone with an actual brain rather than simply a pair of sun-baked boobs riding above a pair of cheap Italian look-alike heels. There has to be more to the woman than I have plumbed so far. Surely.* He concluded from the front she was comprised quite simply of a garish color display below a frightening hairstyle (or lack of any such style), a pair of watermelons loosely anchored to a petite frame, the first signs of a paunch, all stacked above a pair of platform heels that elevated her above most any man – NBA employees excepted. From the rear he conjectured that her image was, from top to bottom, the West Coast home for split-ends, a bubble butt, and platform heels. *You know,* he thought*, she may have chosen those shoes well as they are the one constant in her appearance.* He paused to reflect momentarily as his gaze followed a voluptuous coed stride-for-stride as her backside twitched its way across campus – a cell phone firmly implanted into her head. "*I swear*," he muttered to himself, "*if skirts get any shorter, these little princesses will have more cheeks to powder before they strut around trying to destroy a man's self-confidence. . . hmmm, been there, done that.*"

"Where was I? Oh yes... what to do about Brenda."

Hughes picked up a text on Abnormal Psychology, leafed it open to some meaningless location, threw his loafers onto the desk and assumed the proper posture just in case that sniveling little Steingrit came snooping around. The trick on this overheated day would be to come up with a new plan of attack before, or after, he fell asleep behind the seven hundred page text that often fronted for Hughes' lack of motivation. The real trick would be to not drop the book to the floor and have his head wag over backwards, his mouth agape and emitting a log-sawing sound like a mill in the north of Maine. Steingrit had interrupted that little piece of heaven all too often and had only ugly things to say as Hughes' slobbers dribbled off his chin and had formed a large wet spot on an already stained and spotted shirt.

Inevitability being what it is, the trumpeting sound of the pugnacious and stout Chairman of the University Chancellor, Academic Qualifications Review Panel, broke Hughes from a sound interlude into which he had slipped as he fleeted away from reality. He was somewhere on a Caribbean island sipping a rum-laced drink and smiling at the sarong-clad virgins as they passed his umbrella on a pristine stretch of white sand. As Steingrit burst onto the scene, the seven hundred page text flew as if it had sprouted wings and Hughes nearly did as well as his swivel rocker launched him butt over bifocals in a backward arc. *"Shit! Not again."*

"Oh! Herr Steingrit, I mean, Professor Steingrit, sir, I was just developing a new stratagem for the interview procedures with the subject."

"Yes, I could see your progress each time you snorted. Get on it Hughes or I swear to you I'll revoke your

university club privileges and reduce your charge account level at the bookstore."

"You wouldn't!" an exercised Hughes shot back.

Embarrass us with a botched study and I'll crucify you. Now, I've got to go join Helen, err I mean, Dr. Brighthurst and that graduate assistant of yours. He wants to talk to me about something." Pausing for effect, he continued, " Dennis, I think his name is."

"Yes, I'm sure you have your hands full with her, figuratively speaking, of course. As for Dennis. . . I'm sure he'd like you to get a handful, if you get my drift."

"Hughes, just think of me as a Doberman Pincer and you're wearing Milk Bone underwear. It's just a matter of time."

The Letter

"Dear Brenda.   Let me begin this letter by apologizing that our sessions have not gone well so far and pledge to you my sincere commitment that I will try to make our time together more productive.

I am under a great deal of pressure to conduct a series of interviews with you and write a paper explaining the course of your life – the hope is, that there are some lessons you/ve learned that might prove to help other girls facing some of the difficulties you have undergone.

If I am to continue to pay you the fifty dollars per session I have to get very direct responses to my questions. Where is this headed, you ask? Well, I need to learn a great many details about your childhood and your family, about your days in school and growing up, your teen years, relationships with your father, boyfriends and then how and why you got started in the 'adult entertainment industry.' I also need to know what it was like as a 'model' and being in

films, what the people were like, what you did with your time, how much you made and where it has led you.

I know this is a lot to deal with but we will take each of my topics one at a time and explore them.

I promise, as I said, to be understanding.

I have attached a questionnaire that will help you think through what we will talk about at our next session. I will see you at your 'Hollywood Shangri La', as you put it, next Tuesday at one.

Sincerely. Malcolm Hughes, Ph.D.

p.s. I hope you will stop your comments about my clothes."

Reality

Bright sunlight splashed throughout the room as if it were a police interrogation facility. The tattered curtains hung scarred by ravelings and snags and the louvered blinds – some bent, some absent – shed light like a sieve.

"Oh Jesus, Debbie, would you look at these *freakin* questions." Brenda looked up from the multi-page questionnaire sent by Dr. Hughes. "This is what that asshole wants to talk about? I thought he wanted to get kinky, you know, couldn't do it anymore so he just likes to talk through a fantasy. But this! What does the man want?"

Debbie took the questionnaire from Brenda and stepped into the doorway where the light shone in a more consistent swath across the papers. Her head twisted back and forth as she seemingly read through the questions. When she was finished she flipped them back into their order and said to Brenda, "no problem Sweetie. You were the Queen of Porn – you can do anything after that experience. Besides you can do this sitting up – you don't have to lie down or get into some

ridiculous position. And, you get fifty dollars for each of the sessions. The trick for you, no pun intended, is to drag this out long enough to make sure you get the most money possible. Give him enough each time to keep that scrawny twit happy and beggin' for more."

"God... you're good Debbie. You should have been my manager. As it was, the one I had got me, my money, and paid for nothing – I paid him to take everything away from me." Brenda lamented the shortcomings of being vulnerable, having a penchant for revealing clothes that highlighted breasts large enough to provide shade for her feet and legs.

"Do you think I should tell him the truth when he asks these questions?'

Debbie puzzled over the question for a moment suggesting at least a marginally greater capacity for deductive reasoning than possessed by the woman across from her – the woman thought of as a giant pair of boobs floating and jiggling above a pair of fake Italian platform shoes.

"Yeah. I do. What the hell is it going to hurt? It says right here that all the responses will be used without reference to the individual – you being the individual. Besides, you couldn't make up a story that would rival your life. Honey, you've had a pretty screwed up life. It might make you feel nice if someone read all this when the geeky professor is all done and actually ended up thinking of you as a person rather than the owner of those things." Debbie nodded with her head in the direction of Brenda's chest as she did so.

A thump, thump, thump Latin beat trumpeted its way around the corner from Hollywood Boulevard to Ivan – a ghetto blaster balanced on the shoulder of a veritable billboard

of human skin as two of East LA's finest made their way to their Chev-V. Into the rancorous background Debbie winced and softly uttered, "I always thought these were the greatest but I don't think they ever really got me what I want in life." Brenda turned from her friend and stood eyeing her image in the full length mirror that was mounted in the only room of the deteriorating studio apartment. It didn't take a carnival convex mirror to make her look disproportionately top heavy.

"What do you want from life Brenda?" Debbie purred as she stepped up behind Brenda and wrapped her arms around the shoulders of her one and only friend. She nuzzled her chin into the back of Brenda's neck and they both looked at the image before them. "Do you know what you want Brenda?" The effervescence and confidence was gone from her voice. "What would make you happy, Brenda? Really happy." The sadness that her voice conveyed seemed to move between their two bodies like an electric current that joined them.

"I thought I knew. I was happy, I thought. I was making a lot of money. I had great looking men making love to me. Everyone at the photo shoots and on the sets of the video production always seemed to respect me. I was somebody."

Debbie hugged Brenda's shoulders tighter. "No honey, you *had* a body and everyone wanted it. All those good looking guys as you put it wanted your body and the people behind the scenes wanted what your body would bring them. None of them gave a damn about you. . . not as a person. Not as the beautiful lady you are."

A tear trickled down Brenda's left cheek. It was followed immediately by another and another. Brenda and Debbie hugged each other tightly. Brenda was beginning to

40

understand the difference between the fantasy world in which she had been cast and the reality that lurks behind fantasy. If she had been asked to define reality, Brenda would have tried in her own, uneducated manner to explain defeatism and the inevitability that grows from failure.

Early Childhood

"Do you mind if I have a beer while we talk?" asked the nervous former porn queen... well, at least porno princess. Her name had glittered; her body had glittered; but her lack of business acumen had kept her from reigning supreme.

"No, Brenda, not if it relaxes you and we can get this going."

The air in the studio apartment that was situated above the Ding Vinh liquor store was stagnant, stale, recycled from the all-too-earthly odors of the street-oriented society of Hollywood. It smelled of things that Dr. Hughes chose not to try to envision. He took a cursory survey of the environment while Brenda found herself an off-brand beer.

The decorating had apparently been done with the use of a grenade and the final designer touches included a pair of mesh nylons drying over a browned lampshade and a pile of soiled clothes were strewn between the one small closet and the bed. The one window in the apartment was obliterated

with stickers with clever messages and with peace symbols. The real message lay in the posters that covered much of the limited wall space. The images of Marlon Brando, Brad Pitt, and George Clooney sent a mixed message to the viewer as to Brenda's interests – all highly successful movie industry icons, but with radically different styles.

Brenda had been across the room getting a beer from the small icebox while Hughes continued to conduct a mental survey of his surroundings. "Ready?" he asked.

Twisting a strand of yellowed hair around a protruding fingernail, Brenda began: "I was born in Terre Haute, Indiana. 1960 was the year. My dad, as I remember him, worked in one of the strip coal mines. He came home about midnight – when he came home. Either they worked sixteen hours a day there and served whiskey for their employees' breaks or he had another life in a tavern somewhere.

When I was five or six, I remember we visited some old people. My mom said I could call the old man 'grandpap' but it was the only time we saw them. My dad and the old man, my grandfather I suppose, got into a bad argument about money. My dad threw a punch at him and stormed out. Mom grabbed me like a sack of potatoes and ran through the door behind him. I don't remember a whole lot about that time of my life. My friend Debbie says that I've buried it. Maybe she's right.

I do remember school, kindergarten I mean," Brenda paused reflectively with a dour look drifting over her face.

"Do you mean the kindergarten class that you attended?"

"No. I just remember the building and asking why I didn't get to go where the other kids were going."

"Well then," Hughes began, "if you didn't attend kindergarten you spent your days with your mother. Home schooling and nurturing like that can be a very positive reinforcement for a young child."

"No, Dr. Hughes, that isn't what I meant at all. I didn't attend kindergarten but I surely didn't spend the days with my mother either. I think she was off boozing most of the time. I played at home by myself. Several times a strange man would leave her bedroom while I was there. I didn't understand it at the time and she said it was uncle somebody. At the time I can recall believing that I had a huge family. My dad had more brothers than some of those men named in the Bible. Later I pieced it together. She died of uterine cancer when I was eleven or twelve. I didn't really have birthday parties so keeping track of time was always a little tough."

Hughes stared straight through Brenda's head looking for meaning to what he was hearing. The answer didn't exist within Brenda's grasp so he stared unconsciously as he tried to comprehend. He had interviewed some down-and-outers before but the picture, pixel by unconnected pixel that Brenda was constructing was looking a little grim.

A melancholy had settled over Brenda. Her childhood was probably a lot worse than she had made it sound and it sounded abysmal. There hadn't been enough love in her family to spread on a piece of toast. Hughes wondered about these failings as he looked at the woman who had once adorned the silver screen at the Pussy Cat theaters and a countless number of video boxes. It seemed that her threadbare existence, the proliferation of makeup – too much of the wrong kind in the wrong places – the varicose-veined

44

legs and the out-of-shape body was tied to her childhood and not directly to her "glory" years. Where had she been and what had she done to rise from nothing to something and back again? He continued his silence for a protracted period not asking any questions and fearing the impact of the answers he would hear if he did.

"Enough for one day. I don't want to make you upset. And, we have enough here to cover the early part of your life I think. If not, I can always come back and ask a question or two to fill in gaps as the need arises later."

Brenda lifted her head slightly and attempted a smile. It lasted only momentarily and a melancholy drifted back like the onset of dusk each day. Then Hughes left with a pat to the top of her head.

Junior High

Brenda had slipped into a deep funk during the previous session so Dr. Hughes decided to meet with Brenda at a place that was less oppressive than her little studio apartment.

Hughes caught the Red Line subway downtown not far from his USC campus office and took the glittering new underground train to Hollywood. He had told Brenda on the phone to meet him at the Hollywood / Highland station. They would walk to a small conce-ssionaire along the Hollywood Walk of Fame and talk over an Orange Julius. That would be pleasant, non-intoxicating and maybe she would open up a little without all the remorse from the last visit.

"Ah! There you are Brenda. I was hoping you could find the station okay." Hughes reached forward to take her hand as a welcoming gesture.

"Jeez, doc, I'm short on money and shit out of luck but I'm not stupid. I live three blocks from here," Brenda

retorted with a facial expression that hovered somewhere between friendly and mild hostility. Being talked down to was the thing that she disliked most from people whether university professor or garbage truck driver, she refused to take it from anyone.

After sucking down her second large Orange Julius, Hughes finally ventured into the mottled turmoil that was the life of Brenda.

"Are you telling me your life pretty much skips forward to junior high? You've told me almost nothing about your life to that point." Hughes's eyebrows raised creating several furrows in that area north of his nose and south of where an unkempt mien of stringy hair had previously resided.

"If I remember anything else from the past I'll throw it in when I remember. Now... should I tell you about my time at Junior High?"

"Please. I'll start my tape recorder."

"The biggest events during those years were these." Brenda looked down at the pulchritudinous land of happiness projecting below her chin and above a navel that had gotten lost in time. The twin forty-twos actually had names and some thought they might each have their own zip code. They seemed to *create* one event after another she recalled. Brenda's barely-concealed assets were of mountainous proportion against her tiny frame. "And they're all real, doc."

"I could venture a guess but I think you'd better explain what you mean."

"I was the first girl in my class to get boobs. The girls hated me. You could see them sneering and whispering to each other when I was around. I was never invited to

47

overnights or to join them in anything they did. But that was okay. It hurt but I got even. They had each other and I had all the boys. And I mean *all* the boys. And I had them *right* where I wanted them."

"And where would that have been, Brenda?"

"Right down the top of my sweaters of course. Their hands, their ugly snouts and more.... Sometimes it wasn't fun; sometimes it was even disgusting but I had to do it. I had to control each of them with the promise, as they saw it, and lie as I saw it that they would find the ultimate treasure they were looking for. It was there, sure enough, but I was saving that for the future. Just getting their grubby hands all over the twins was enough for most of them although a few pushed it more. That's when they got a knee in the groin and a slap across the chops. Most importantly, however, they got a threat that there would be no more good times with the twins if they didn't follow the rules. That seemed to work quite well because these things were beauties and the only ones around. I had to lock everyone in before I got some competition. It worked like a dream. I got candy and presents like it was Christmas almost daily. Ohhhh, it really pissed off the other girls and it was wonderful."

"That was your junior high? You've just told me about your boobs.. I mean about your breasts."

"Yes doc that's just what I mean to tell you. And if it weren't for the twins I would have been held back and no high school."

Hughes rolled his head backward and looked up at what would have been the sky in most cities. In Los Angeles, however, it was the diffusion of billions of particles of particulate matter emitted from the exhaust of automobiles

that slowly choked everything and everyone to death when exposed to it enough. "Explain, please."

"The boys were getting the twins, several of my teachers were getting the whole package. Passing me to high school was a small payment in return."

Pussy Kat Theater

Brenda stood watching the wobbly-kneed professor scurry across the street to return to the Metro station. Traffic was lighter than usual. That meant that there were only one hundred or so SUV's per city block of traffic as opposed to normal conditions. Whether or not Los Angeles was the SUV capital of the world had not been determined but SUV's were the rage and no one follows fads like Angelinos.

Brenda watched the traffic swish by – all the high profile individuals, each with a cell phone attached to the side of his or her head, only occasionally watching traffic conditions. She looked longingly at the parade. These were people of means, people with families and loved ones. These were people with homes, not studio apartments above Vietnamese liquor stores. She sighed, turned and began her trek down the boulevard back toward the hovel she called home and happily referred to as *Shangri La*.

Brenda combined casual window-shopping with star-struck stares at the images implanted in the sidewalk of former

entertainment greats as she strolled along. A vendor hawking souvenirs to the busloads of tourists, mostly Japanese, caught Brenda's attention. She turned her gaze to the storefront displays. Prominent in the window was a black-and-white, twenty-four by thirty-six inch poster of Marlon Brando. It was a knock-off from Brando's defining role - On the Water Front. It was captioned, "... *I could have been somebody*." The parody was a reflection on the highly successful career of the aging actor.

I could have been somebody too, she spoke, just above a whisper. Brenda's thought process had floated along the Boulevard stacked above her platform heels and above the thunderous bounce of the twins. However, her happiness was barometric – one could see it change almost instantaneously given an improper catalyst or comment. The ebullient bounce along the boulevard slowed to a drag. The funk was returning. Brenda's life had an obvious volatility. Many in Hollywood, she thought, had tenuous life stories. Most ended slumped around a blunted needle, some raped and dumped into a trash dumpster or off the side of Angeles Crest Highway, the road that snakes it way through the mountains overhanging the greater Los Angeles area. *Maybe I don't have it so bad after all," she thought. "How many of my friends from the business ended up taking an OD to end their career. So much for the glamour of the sex-for-hire industry that splashed its trade across silver screens and television screens compliments of VHS and DVD.* If it weren't for all these letter combinations she wouldn't have made so much money – for other people.

"Screw it!" she barked aloud. People turned from their docility to see what had interrupted their self-centered world - a crazy woman, obviously, bantering and carrying on in some manner that clearly displayed the absence of mental or moral control.

"Screw all of you too!" she continued, once she realized she had become the focus of so much attention. "For that matter, I may have already done that – at least to the men." She laughed, a banter that would have bordered on a professional psychiatrist's definition of schizophrenic, manic-depressive behavior. More stares. "Enough of this shit and all these people who are clueless."

The day was either typically dismal, if you were an Angeleno, or wonderfully warm and full of promise and great curiosities if you were the typical tourist. In the Midwest where Brenda grew up, and out, the weather at this time of year could be truly oppressive. The temperature could fluctuate across the landscape like the movement of a gazelle eluding a hungry lioness. Worse yet was the humidity – it could suck the body's water through the microscopic pores of the skin as if it were a sieve. Here in Hollywood, the temperature seldom varied, it only rained a small amount and then only during a specific, limited period, and a thunderstorm was about as common as a virgin at a Grateful Dead concert. The sky was not blue; it was not gray. It was some undefined color created by the same crud in the sky that tarnished the stars on the Hollywood Walk of Fame. A girl's best friend, next to birth control, would be sun block. The opaque parchment-colored haze of the sky would facilitate a burn and the threat of melanoma faster than any Hollywood tanning salon.

Brenda walked with a purpose – she was going home. She needed a pick-me-up to work her way out of the all-too-frequent depression that crowded her life into a whirling a series of highs and lows.

Home. Actually the Pussy Cat Theater on Hollywood Boulevard, that was home as often as not. She often came here to relive her greatest moments. Yes, she was home now. Things would get better. She gave her ticket stub to the attendant and took a back row seat. The theater was playing a retrospective, of sorts – twenty-four hours of the best films of Brenda Marlow, Brenda's screen name. Where better to be, what better to be doing? There would be a tomorrow, a happy tomorrow.

So Much for Perversion

The theater was dark but the images immutable – old men, rag poor men, young men, sex-starved men, looking for a fix even if only on celluloid. Some looked around to make contact. Others were slid low into their off-aisle seats.

Brenda had slipped unobtrusively into the last row of seats as quietly as possible. She had come into this sanctuary from reality to solve her own problem, not that of some poor slob who had his hand wrapped around unrealized anxieties.

The dim lighting flickered as the film leader fed through the projector. No smoking in the theater. No eating in the theater. These were messages that conveyed the desire to achieve acceptable social behavior of those in attendance. The odd acrid odor that permeated all available air in the theater conveyed a certain familiarity but which offered a disgusting and near-nauseating suggestion of a behavioral pattern not covered by the screen's messages. No message, however, to indicate no self-abuse. for the lack of a better term.

Brenda knew the odor. That very odor had been part of her professional existence and now was being regenerated by her own screen presence. Regardless, it was nonetheless distasteful.

The offers for popcorn and soft drinks had ended and the previews had finally concluded. There she was – ten years younger, or was it fifteen? A forgettable title spanned across those assets that the assembled degenerates waited and lusted to see. Finally. She stood proudly, front and center on the screen, hands on hips, ballooning out of the top of a sprayed-on red dress that barely covered her varioius objects of desire. She was muttering something on the screen to two men who lay limply across the disheveled bed, their physiques exhausted and their faces blank of expression.

Brenda began to beam. The image she watched jiggled and bounced voluptuously strutting from the bedroom. Damn she looked good – a sexual goddess. No wonder all the men in this theater and all those theaters across the country had their self-realized sexual encounter with her.

As one scene dissolved into another Brenda's eyes glassed over from memories that fueled her passions. Her emotions ran the gamut of excitement, nostalgia and pride. Twinges of new passion caused her to twitch and yearn to quell that lust with a powerfully-built young stud but those randomly distributed throughout the aging theater didn't match that trait. The men in the theater were now what she had come to expect as potential partners – overweight, unshaven, rumpled clothing, all were unclean and many doubtlessly carried one form of social disease or another.

Brenda's myopic self-assessment of her on-screen grandeur had diminished her peripheral concentration. Brenda had been unaware of the salamander-like move of a middle-

aged down-and-outer as he slipped into the seat next to her. The man hadn't recognized Brenda as the persona on the screen, he had been drawn by the presence of the singular outlet for his male release. His focus was particular and elevating his level of anxiety. He responded to the chemical perturbations his body generated by reaching forward with his hand to envelope one of Brenda's anatomical excesses. The squeeze was unexpected and immediately frightening. It also was not tender or gentle but did provoke an abrupt response from Brenda who swung her nearest arm in a half-arc smashing the point of her elbow firmly in the eye socket of the stunned pervert. The response was predictably loud and disrupting to all those who were otherwise engrossed in their own fantasies.

Brenda bolted from the duct-taped leatherette seat as if a firecracker had just torn at her backside. She was out of the theater and into the harsh illumination that sufficed for sunlight in one burst of energy. She didn't need that kind of provocation. When she had sex she would determine where and when and with whom.

Sex. What a pleasant thought. Had it been the movie that reinvigorated her passions? Had the disgusting individual in the theater generated some sort of animal passion in her? She wasn't sure but there was a need that now had to be satisfied. Who? How would she find someone, the right someone who was worthy of all that she had to offer? Brenda wrestled with her point of philosophical distraction as she bounced her way along the boulevard toward Ivar Street.

The question was made moot when Brenda's focus was abruptly shattered by a twentyish creation of virulence striding quickly from one of the boulevard stores. "Perdóndeme Seniorita! I beg your pardon, I mean. I'm very sorry. I didn't mean to run into you so hard. Actually, I didn't

mean to run into you at all," stumbled the muscled Hispanic in his best attempt at the English language. His "T" shirt which alluded to the Hard Rock Café in Honolulu was drawn skin-tight and exposed a set of biceps that were labeled with a pair of tattoos that said "Gold's" on the left and "Jim" on the right. Apparently the tattoo artist was not an aficionado of the bodybuilding phenomenon that controlled the entire social mindset of Southern California. To further detract from the tattoo artist's resume, he most likely had not finished grade school. "I beg your pardon," repeated the Latino. "Are you hurt… is there anything I can do?"

"Actually, there might be. Walk me home and we'll talk about it."

The two ambled on down the boulevard. Brenda slid her arm in through that of the young man and pressed herself closely so that her amplitude struck a nerve and redirected the focus of the young man – just like all those who watched the silver screen at the Pussy Cat.

The Twins had once again worked their magic.

Every Pervert Needs a Minox

His life seemed to be governed by the weather as much as anything. Hughes loved the warmth of southern California. It was a far cry from his native Nacogdoches, Texas. He'd been away from that lost corner of rudimentary civilization for a long time and acclimated keenly to the advances that the Golden State offered. Considering his penchant for eyeing young women he thought he was in heaven, not just Los Angeles.

The decision to relocate from Texas where he received his academic training at Stephen F. Austin State University and his doctoral work at the University of Texas had been easy – he had been ready to move on.

This was one of those days, a day that he had realized that he had made the right decision to head for the land of the perfect body. While he was ostracized for his puny form and his complete lack of taste in clothing, he nonetheless had a

focus on young women that bordered on the perverse. The role of university professor was ideally suited for Hughes' prurient interests. He had thought at one point that being an L.A. County lifeguard would offer him even greater opportunities to satisfy his urgings but he was such a dismal excuse for physical fitness that was not an option. Then there was the time he considered working in the porno industry – admittedly, it was a fleeting thought. He wasn't sure what he'd do. He had no expertise as a cameraman or sound technician. He didn't know the people in the industry so producing was out of the question and he figured the only way to direct was by example and that would be like a caterer eating the trays of finger foods to prove their edible. The ultimate consideration. . . performing. . . well that would be heaven-sent. However, his frequency at the shady theaters, combined with his collection of prurient magazines provided him with the realization that there was a certain physical expectation. One needed a large key to open the locks so lasciviously displayed on screen. Hughes didn't possess such a master key; he held only a skeleton key.

Today was the epitome of the southern California's best offering. The sun was actually visible, perched high in a uniformly powder blue sky. It was cloudless and the dry heat was hovering in the low nineties. *This ought to bring out the skimpy outfits*, Hughes thought to himself. *I'll take my notebook and my Minox camera over to the outdoor pool – this'll be better than the beach. None of that damn sand.*

Hughes traipsed down the institutionally-decorated hallway with his miniature camera tucked into his shirt pocket protector and a notepad about his interviews with Brenda tucked under his arm. He unwittingly slipped his shades on as he quietly closed his door. The Ray Bans made the gloomy hallway so dark that he hadn't seen Drs. Steingrit and Brighthurst conducting a mutual grope inside the janitor's closet. Instead, he smacked right into the opened door causing a small lump to immediately protrude on his forehead and two silly-looking middle aged frumps to begin clearing their throats and straightening their clothes.

"Goddamn you Hughes, you pernicious bastard."

"Oh! Was that you, Dr. Steingrit? I hadn't noticed. Nice day outside... what are you doing in a closet?"

Off he went, his scrawny ass hidden among the combined stripes and vivid colors of a horrendously designed pair of Bermuda shorts. His black shoes and white socks rounded out a combination that would cause a gay man to run screaming into the night.

Malcolm Hughes had perfected the art of looking as if he were reading a report while simultaneously snapping away with his spy camera. So successful was he that he had filled scrapbooks with his many pictures of scantily-clad coeds all taken surreptitiously, of course. But then... Hughes had never met Inga, a star athlete on the women's track team who had come to USC from Scandinavia. Using her conference championship form for shot-putting she shoved the little Minox damn near down to Hughes Adams-appled throat. She left a second parting shot, "if you ever show up at this facility again, I'll shove that goofy little camera somewhere else!"

Hughes' left immediately – crushed. His best form of entertainment had just been ripped away much like Shaquille O'Neal taking the basketball away from Billy Bardy (the midget actor). No amount of Viagara would cure the male-numbing impact that the blonde shot-putter had just destroyed.

"Oh shit. I suppose Brenda is looking a little better.
Maybe I'd better focus on this at home."

Poker Revenue

"So, what will it be today Professor? More about the twins?"

"No. I have no interest in those, per se. It's your life I'm interested in... what caused you to take the path that you led." Hughes looked from his notes to the Twins, to his notes, to the Twins, to his notes, to the Twins – a thousand times before actually emitting a sound higher than the guttural moan that welled from within him.

"If that's true why do you keep staring and having to wipe your lower lip? Huh?"

"Never mind that. It's a condition I have."

"Yeah, I know, and that condition is called horny."

Stirring uneasily in the chair opposite the front door to Brenda's studio apartment, Hughes sat beneath the thirty-six by forty-eight inch images of Marlon Brando, Brad Pitt, and George Clooney. No greater injustice had ever befallen

any of these three screen icons that to have the likes of Malcolm Hughes, Ph.D. sitting as if cradled by their likenesses. The stark contrast between their incomparable good looks, sophistication, and romantic symbolism was temporarily lost as Hughes' scraggy appearance and dull-witted self-indulgence spoke in front of the three icons.

"Now. Tell me about your relationship with your mother and father." That is what Hughes said. What Brenda heard was, "Hi... Brenda. My name is Brad Pitt. I've heard a lot of wonderful things about you. I thought we might have dinner tonight at my favorite restaurant in Beverly Hills and then you can show me how a man is supposed to be made love to." Her eyes were targeted about twelve inches above Hughes' yakking mouth and her mind was in Brad Pitt's bedroom. Unfortunately for Brenda some sequence of what Hughes had bantered on about had slipped through the enchantment she had built for herself with who she knew to be the sexiest man alive.

"What? What did you say about my mother?"

After long minutes of jockeying back-and-forth trying to establish a level playing field from which to move his psychological survey forward, Hughes seemed to finally make some headway and get Brenda on course.

"I'm afraid Dr. Hughes, that using the words 'relationship' and 'mother and father' in the same sentence is a little inappropriate."

"And why so, my dear?"

"Quite simply we had no relationship. We had the ultimate dysfunctional family. I was the unfortunate result of a night of lust that followed a hard day of drinking. . . on both

their parts. She was too stupid to know she had been knocked-up and then too frightened to have an abortion. So I popped out eight months later, not as a love child but as a complete accident. Think of it, I'm the product of raw lust between some drunken bastard and a woman who probably had as many men as the great film icon John Hobes had had women."

"John Hobes... film star? Really?"

"Oh yes, Dr. Hughes, you should have known him. He was wonderful – so talented and soooo big. So damn big. Clit, G-Spot be damned. He rang the bells deep, and I mean deep, within the knave of my sanctuary, metaphorically speaking of course." Brenda paused, her eyes slid shut and a smile welled from deep within the knave she spoke of. She was again at peace within herself and then continued. "Oh... I miss him so."

Hughes knew of the film star, as Brenda referred to him. He had been to the Pussy Kat Theater a few times himself and had an enviable collection of VHS tapes – located where no one from the university was ever likely to find them, of course. He couldn't help but quickly do some mental arithmetic subtracting his own personal dimensions from that of the over-dosed actor. All he could compute were negative numbers so he tried quickly to rid the image from his mind.

"So you had no relationship with your parents?"

"I wasn't speaking of my parents." A punctilious expression accented her face as she drew a bead on the man who seemed to keep pulling her from happy reunions. "How do you possibly keep your job, Doctor Hughes? You must have really worked hard to earn that degree of yours. You added that up about my parents real quick like." A look of frustration started to overpower the former actress's ability to

remain in control. "I was shuffled away while my mother would have sex in our house with any guy she could find. When I was young she would try to conceal the situation referring to them as 'uncle' but as time went on she just blew past me tearing at her clothes as she ran for the bedroom and shouting to me to 'get the hell out.' By the time I was fourteen I was basically turning tricks for my dad's friends. They would sit around and play cards, stink up the house with cigar smoke, swear like sailors and keep asking me to bring them another beer. After a while I knew it wasn't the beer they wanted. I was touched here and there all over but it was their eyes as they looked at my body that made me so uncomfortable. Then, as a card game would wrap up, someone would win and he would come throw his drunken arms around me and start shooting his hands inside my blouse. My dad would come over and keep telling me how it was necessary because he had just lost a lot of money to this guy or that and if I wanted to keep living there, I would help out. After all, he would say, I didn't have a job and had to help out some way or the other. So.. I would end up having sex with all of his card-playing cronies each time they got together and I was covering my dad's inability to figure out how to play poker."

"Oh." Hughes paused lost for words. "I see," he said dropping his pinched face toward his notebook.

"No. I sincerely doubt that you do see. Imagine for a moment being a young teenage girl wanting to be like all the other girls but having your father use you like a cheap whore."

Hughes' mind spun in a different direction. "I always thought it would have been better to be a girl." His thoughts conveyed his sentiments as if he were wearing them on his sleeve.

"I think we're done today Dr. Hughes. Will you please leave?"

The dumbfounded Hughes rose slowly scattering his notes as he did so. He choked out a variety of comments, probably inappropriate attempts to mollify the situation and provide comfort to the woman he had once again offended.

"I've never met anyone with as little sensitivity to another person's needs as you . . . and you're supposed to be this superior genius to understand human psychology. Get out! Just get out!"

Debbie's Ire

Things were eventually smoothed over, not because Hughes was a "silver-tongued" devil, but because Brenda's best and only friend Debbie intervened in a face-to-face showdown with the obstreperous Hughes. It was not Debbie's style to mince words especially when it came to defending her soul mate.

"You are supposed to be an educated man, Dr. Hughes. Show it. Okay?" In recalling the episode later, Hughes would swear that he saw fangs protrude as punctuations to each intimidating jolt to his male ego. "So far all you have managed to do is send Brenda into a rather inglorious state of depression. She's very upset. Just thinking about her childhood is painful but to have you pass judgment on her because it is not acceptable to your way of thinking is inconceivable," Debbie blurted in a single gust of bourbon-breath.

Dumbfounded, Hughes sat in his office-empire aghast that someone so clearly beneath his status should have the audacity to lecture him was absurd. He considered rising from his swivel rocker – the office chair with a spring that Hughes thought had been installed by some sadistic proctologist. Hughes eyed the sleazy-looking girl from top to bottom, literally. On reflection and in consideration of the time-honored value of self-preservation, Hughes adjudged that the girl would no doubt knee him in the groin given the chance. That would, of course, end his hopes for any advances that the back of his mind had been entertaining as he ogled her form. She looked street tough and he ended any consideration of a confrontation with a whimper, "whatever."

"Whatever, my ass, you degenerated amalgam of dysfunctional genes. You will begin to treat Brenda like a lady. She deserves it." Debbie continued her romp across the ego of the fidgeting professor who, education notwithstanding, had no meaningful retort. Instead, he tended to focus more on covering his genitals with a text book as a precaution to a sneak attack by the wild-eyed woman who had descended upon his sacrosanct domain.

"Lady! She's a former porno actress and hooker. Why in the hell does that deserve such distinction? And if you impugn my credentials once again this is all off. I will be done with that aging eyesore once and for all."

Debbie rose from her chair, her shrill voice had long since shaken the quietude of academia and Bower's Hall. Now the lithesome brunette was at her virulent best; the professor had awakened her innermost appetite for vengeance. One could almost see her nails extend as if for an attack, saliva glistening on her lips, whetting for the kill.

"I've done some checking on you, Mr. High-and-Mighty Professor. You have to use Brenda because you're running out of time and your grant is all that keeps you on the staff here. Yes, I too have friends in high places or in your case low places."

Hughes felt his decorum wilt like melting ice cream. His bravado had been a misplaced sense of power that he only rented and did not own.

"Perhaps I was hasty."

"Perhaps you're a complete asshole and have no concept of how to treat people."

The tweed jacket was becoming increasing a personal inferno for the embarrassed and humiliated instructor of psychology. Hughes wondered in a flash of awareness that perhaps the trollop across from him was a better psychologist that he, the chairman of the esteemed Psychology Department at the renowned University of Southern Calif-ornia. There would be no way to live this down after his earlier defeats at the hands of Brenda and the humiliation at the university swimming pool with that mannish Swede who had threatened to emasculate him.

"Okay. Let's just say that I give Brenda another chance. Will that get you to calm down?"

Debbie's eyes appeared to sink to a place deep in her skull as her facial composition took on an animal image - her eyes projected as two deep-seated red beads glaring at a prey about to be devoured. She heaved her right arm back and snapped it forward with the tenacity of a tigress killing a newborn gazelle. The normally slow-witted, stodgy-moving demeanor of Hughes was instantly replaced with an

uncharacteristic jolt of adrenalin that propelled him backward to avoid the sting of the she-devil's claws. In doing so Hughes upset the tedious balance of the overage swivel rocker with the proctologic spring and performed a reverse flip that would have honored most Olympians. As his glasses flew in one direction his books and papers were propelled in another. The sudden strain on the tweed cloth of his pants sent a ripping sound resembling a zipper being drawn full length. His pants were torn asunder from the bottom of the fly circumnavigating his crotch to his belt line in the back. His unwashed once white briefs were now on display. "Oh, shiiiiit," shrieked the surprised Hughes.

"Yes. I think I see signs of just that Dr. Hughes. Do we have an agreement?"

"Yes. Yes. Just get out of my office. I'll be nice to the... I'll be nice to Brenda."

An ear-to-ear smile was emerging on Debbie as she pirouetted and pranced out like the cat that had eaten the canary, turning one more time she drove the final nail into Hughes' coffin. "From here forward, the fee is now $100 per session. I have NO doubt as to your agreement."

Pieces of the Puzzle

As he read and re-read his notes and flitted through his taped recordings, Hughes was amassing a picture of Brenda's background that began to fill in the cells in his paint-by-numbers approach to psycho analysis.

Brenda's story had not been a pretty one. Not only was she born as the result of drunken savagery she was born prematurely and not without complications due to the drinking and drugging on the part of her mother.

The love that a newborn receives, typically, was conspicuously absent from the relationship with her mother. Even though he never openly claimed to be her father, the man was living testimony that erectile dysfunction wasn't necessarily a bad condition.

A loved child is a very positive reality within God's world. An unloved child is an unfortunate consequence from time to time. A child despised for having been born is beyond comprehension. Welcome to the world, Brenda. . . .

Mr. Disper, Brenda's father, had precipitated the latter condition. It didn't matter much, however. He was seldom around and too drunk to notice most of the time when he did show up. He had insisted that the child be given the name Brenda much to the exasperation of his common law wife. Brenda had been the name of a former girlfriend; Brenda's mother was constantly scorned for not measuring up to the former girlfriend.

Before Brenda had even had her third birthday, the drunken wanderer would lock the small child in a closet for crying or having a wet diaper. The dark closet generated anxiety and fear and the crying only increased. This brought fist pounding thuds to the door until the man's hands were raw.

Attempts on the part of neighbors to intervene in behalf of the child had proved inconsequential and the County's Child Services Department had been unable to establish a solid set of grounds for removing the child because the father could never be found to interview and the mother was at once loving and thoughtful even though the arms that held the child were punctuated with tracks of needle marks from one end to the other.

Brenda's mother, Sylvia, had tried to be a mother – at least when it was convenient and she was sober. She had fed Brenda as a baby and later as a young child; she had even changed a diaper from time to time. However, the diapers would remain wet on the child for countless hours before being removed – the inflamed rashes never seemed to go away.

Slowly the baby became a young child and the child grew in spite of the conditions thrust upon it. Perhaps it was God's way of getting even by not offering them the easy way

72

out by having the child simply die. They were forced to continue to face Brenda and tend to her needs one way or the other.

As the young child grew enough to lose the moniker "young" and was just a child, the addict who had spawned the child found a new pleasure to add to his deviant behavior. For a fee, his drinking buddies could come to his apartment and see the child in ways that can only be described as criminal and demonstrative of a sickness and perversity held by only the lowliest of humanity. The occasional visitors to the Disper apartment would gape and fondle and then satisfy their own sick needs. The child understood none of this but had taken her first steps, albeit not by choice, to becoming a sexual vehicle for men's most prurient interests. This was the beginning of a life to be filled with emptiness and despair but one that would provide meaning to those who otherwise had no life or ability to function in society. Yes, welcome to the world, Brenda.

The Code of Ethics

Hidden within the recesses of his cluttered office, Hughes reflected on his jottings as he sat perched atop a tome entitled, *The Code of Ethics: Professionalism within the Realm of Psychoanalytic Analysis*. The book was finally providing him with some benefit – it blunted the business end of the spring that had worked its way through the chair and had become the equivalent of a proctologists' probe. Otherwise, the book was of no particular value. Hughes had his own set of values that guided his professional activities; he answered to a higher authority, a position he often proffered to his colleagues. *Books like this butt saver under me are intended for the uninitiated, those without the higher calling who can't see how those of us who so thoroughly understand the human mind and the motivations that guide human interaction. . .* Hughes' mental wanderings dribbled off without conclusion. His self-aggrandizement while usually comforting caused conflict with another cerebral fart that was on the verge of taking shape.

Brenda! What in the hell do I do with this problem. It seemed so simple at the beginning; find some down-and-outer who would be good for a few freebies, some prime time with my Minox and then write a paper about some meaningless life about which no one would give a damn. Plan A hasn't worked quite as I would have intended, I must admit. She's busted my cajones on more than one occasion, embarrassed me, and, God forbid, even caused me some tremulous moments thinking about my ascendancy within my profession.

I will see her just a couple more times and round out her miserable life; I haven't gotten to the point of her insinuation into the porn industry as yet and where that led. These will be the most critical elements of my work.

This woman has loser written all over her; what a pathetic case.

Hughes had sat for nearly an hour, pen in hand, assessing his thoughts as to how to advance his research and justify a billing to the U.S. Department of Education. They were such sticklers for details – wanting to see actual effort expended and the results. *Damn such narrow minded people anyway.*

About this time one of the professor's students in his 101 class on human interactions stepped into the intellectual sepulcher that was his office. Final exams were nearing and here was the primary reason Malcolm Hughes had elected to enter the university teaching profession: blonde, obviously from a moneyed-family, a face so stunning that Jennifer Anniston would have blushed, a body that had surely been sculpted by a Hollywood producer, and an outfit so revealing that Hughes could only think of the "Emperor's new clothes."

The professor babbled a welcome that was nominally intelligible as he dug into his pocket to extract his ever-present Minox camera and set it unobtrusively on the corner of his desk for ease of use. The professor's intent was not lost on the coed who had been pre-warned of the behavioral pattern to expect. The young woman responded by smiling even more warmly and crossing her legs in a manner that a see-through thong became abundantly evident. Hughes rose from his chair to extend his hand, not as a welcome to his office, but to make contact with her warm flesh. Cause and effect: the suppressed spring in his chair uncoiled and propelled the useless text across the room providing sufficient distraction that Hughes' leering gestures were muted.

The coed, fully aware of her power, re-crossed her legs in the opposite direction flashing more with each movement. Following the obvious display came the soft and ingenuous question to the god of grades. "Professor Hughes. . . I seem to be having some difficulty in your class. . . ."

"How would you know Miss Hunter, my records show that you've only showed up twice so far this semester?"

"Professor Hughes. . . I'd do anything to get a <u>good</u> grade in your class. . . just <u>anything</u>. Do you <u>understand</u>?" As Hughes lower jaw began to sag from the lack of a coherent thought the young woman rose and pushed the office door closed and snapped the lock with a moment-shattering CLICK.

The young woman floated back through the space between them, her jewels spilling from her treasure chest, so to speak. Sliding her hands up each of Hughes' thighs she knelt in between his splayed legs. "Anything. Anything at all." Ziiiiiiip !

Hughes had already snapped a dozen Minox pictures by the time the coed could no longer speak. "I suppose this is what psychology is all about in its most fundamental form — finding a means of expression to achieve one's ambitions and self-fulfillment.   Yes, Ms. Hunter, this is a perfectly acceptable way by which to express your inner needs. This is psychology Ms. Hunter in its most rudimentary form.   You pass!."

Working Toward Closure

The day following that which affixed a permanent smile to the face of the pseudo-intellectual aberration, Malcolm Hughes, was overcast and dreary. No, not rain, not in Southern California – that was a statistical impossibility. The Santa Ana winds had blown in from the deserts with a vengeance bringing clouds of dirt and sand suspended in a cloud-like formation that darkened the skies and the demeanor of the effervescent Hughes. He could hardly sleep following Ms. Hunter's initiation into the select group of students who never attended class, took no examinations and were compensated with the grade of "A."

Hughes caught the Blue Line light rail train jumping off at Seventh and Flower Streets, changed levels and grabbed the Red Line subway out to Hollywood.

It took a concerted effort for Hughes to finesse his way past the old Vietnamese liquor store owner who was a self-styled gatekeeper for his upstairs renter. Ding Vinh had come to this country following the war. Contrary to U.S. State Department policy that provided for the incorporation of a

huge number of displaced Vietnamese, those who had suffered at the hands of the enemy and those who had no homes or livelihood because of our intervention in their country, Ding Vinh had actually been VC and had killed numerous GIs during the war. Ding Vinh was flown to the U.S. at State Department expense – a branch of our government typically characterized as "clueless."

"Brenda. I'm glad you're home. Could we talk for a little while? I guarantee that I will be on my best behavior and say nothing to offend you." Hughes paused for dramatic effect followed by an ingenuous, "Please."

Brenda stood in the doorway holding the lacerated screen open with her left arm and caused her unbelted housecoat to hang openly. One of the Twins had decided to come out for a look to see who was at the door as well. Peering past the obvious, Hughes scanned the apartment for what had apparently been a night of debauchery. For her part, Brenda's hair looked as if she had held a metal fork in an outlet as the means by which to achieve her grooming. Her makeup was smeared, the wrong shades, running, and always in considerable excess.

Squinting at the refracted image through the screen door, Hughes asked his subject if he might come in and continue with another of his interviews. He was met with a reluctant affirmative but punctuated with an "okay, but I have to pee first." Hughes cracked a slight smile and stepped in brushing past the peaking Twin whose large pink eye made contact with the sexually invigorated professor. Yesterday's conquest had returned his self-image of being a sexual god. *Now this. Direct contact with one of the Twins, as she calls them. Yes. This is going to be another good day. Where is that damn Minox when I need it?*

79

A brief respite from the dust-laden air outside for Hughes and a chance to make thirty seconds worth of creative grooming for Brenda set the stage for another of Hughes' sessions.

"Good you're back. . . if I may . . . about your entry into the adult entertainment industry. . . can you tell me how this was performed? How did you get started? . . . respond to a newspaper ad? . . . someone you knew introduced you? . . . What?"

Brenda leaned backward on the couch, throwing one leg over the other, the filmy material of her housecoat not following the leg and leaving her exposed from encrusted lips to swollen ankle. She looked down, snorted slightly, smiled and pulled the door to Hughes' heaven gate closed.

"I was seduced." The words came out without forethought or any encumbering reservations. "No. I was tricked by a slimy son of a bitch." Brenda reached inside the housecoat and scratched across a nipple with her deadly finger nails.

"I had finally broken out of that hellhole in which I lived where my father, such as he was, used me along with letting all his buddies use me. The only sex I ever had was to pay debts. Any thoughts of romance being associated with the sex act were a complete disconnect."

"That's a very interesting choice of words Brenda. I'm quite pleased."

"Yeah, I read it in Cosmo down at the CVS drug store on the Boulevard. Well, anyway, as I was saying, I was just hanging out in crash pads, doin' drugs, whoring, and rolling the occasional derelict for some pocket money.

Nothin' big time but I had to eat. Then one day, this slick-lookin' dude in his black leather pants, skin tight, and chest bursting from beneath a silk shirt walked up to me on the Boulevard. He starts talkin' to me all the while he's starin' at the Twins. I don't think he realized I had a head."

"How did that make you feel? Were you disgusted that someone would take such interest in your body and not you as a person?" asked the academic.

"Are you shittin' me little man? Didn't you hear me say this guy was a real dude. I was doing' quite a bit of starin' of my own. With those pants so tight, I probably couldn't describe him above the waist."

"I see. Go on."

"Rocko says to me, 'lookin' at you, doll, has given me an idea. I'm in the film industry and I think we could make something out of you. . . if you're interested. It would take some work and expense on my part but I see some promise here.' I told him I thought he was lookin' at two promises; he smiled and took a step back and reached for my hand. Quite a gentleman he was – very sweet to me and the sort of lay I had always dreamed about. You've got to remember what my sex life had consisted of to this point."

As she spoke it became evident that she was reliving an important segue in her life as she absentmindedly flicked the index finger nail back and forth over her left nipple.

"That olive-oil boy thoroughly cleaned my pipes before the night was out and sent me to a land that I didn't know existed. It was not a place you'd find advertised in the AAA store down on the Boulevard but it was a place that I thought existed only in fairy tales."

Brenda's body seemed to relax and soften to her environment as her eyes glassed over slightly. "We made love many times that night and for weeks to come while Rocko got me introductions to producers and others. I guess I wasn't completely shocked to hear that the movies would be sex films but then, this is Hollywood. So What? Most every girl who has made it here has showed her goodies or done something using her body to get past that hurdle to stardom. Why would it be any different for me? I could do these things better than anyone else so I figured so if performance were a criterion for success I would have a lock on stardom."

Hughes was hearing about one word in ten but he didn't miss a single stroke of Brenda's finger as it flicked back and forth over the material-covered point of attraction.

"Is this what you want, Professor?" Brenda was trying to draw a conclusion from the discourse she had followed for nearly two hours.

"Yes, huh, yea." Hughes' comments were garbled by the amount of saliva pumping past his tongue and out the corner of his mouth. They remained on two different wave lengths – one having a need for understanding and acceptance and the other not giving a shit about anything except self-gratification at that moment.

Ascendancy

"At first. . . well, I thought it was what they call star quality that got me all my success. But ya know, I think it was the fact that I had to sleep with as many guys off the screen as I did on the screen that got my breaks. I thought about it from time to time – it bothered me. Then one day I decided, what the hell, stardom is stardom. I was a star. I had to scrap my way to the top but by God I was at the top." Brenda finished her dissertation staring straight ahead, affixed on a point of space somewhere above Hughes' left shoulder; her jaw firm and her back rigid as she projected herself from the ailing couch. Hughes, for his part, decided to say nothing. She seemed to have hit a stride and he wanted her to continue to roll while she was in the mood to talk. After all, she was sufficiently moody that anything positive could turn ugly without provocation.

Brenda hesitated as if structuring a sequence of events in her mind. Maybe, however, she needed to conjure a proper spin for those events so as to cast an image that would support her ego.

"They spent a lot of time with me. I almost never had my clothes on but it didn't seem to bother them. In fact, I think they preferred to work with me that way. It didn't seem perfectly natural but they were paying me real good money and I didn't want to rock that boat." A miniscule smile curled at the right of Brenda's lips, casting for the first time a glimpse of a natural dimple in her cheek. It was like an exclamation mark to her natural beauty but a quality generally obscured by the obsessive amount of makeup that she wore. *Perhaps*, Hughes thought, *I should have seen her during her heyday. Maybe I would have found her more attractive then. Maybe she's got some photos of herself during her reign as the Tit Queen of Hollywood.*

Without warning the silence was shattered as Brenda resumed her dissertation quite unexpectedly. Most likely the only silence was that in Hughes' mind where a vacuous condition generally existed without conflict from thought or reason. "They worked with me a great deal to see to it I walked the right way, jiggled the right way that I wore the properly revealing outfits and a lot more. I had makeup artists at my call and hairstylists, cute young boys doing my nails, hands and feet mind you, and a man who I was told was a doctor would check me out on a regular basis. I was never actually convinced he was a doctor. I just think he liked seeing things up real close. He would give me a certificate so I could work that said I didn't have social diseases."

Brenda's eyes remained focused on that meaningless three dimensional cube of space that seemed to possess the history of her professional career. She proceeded to read from the non-existent cube as if it were a hologram suspended in space just over Hughes' shoulder. As abruptly as she had begun the discourse she halted, uncrossed her legs rather unceremoniously and pulled herself from the clutches of the couch. She crossed the room toward the area at the far end of

the space that was non-visually partitioned as her bed chamber. Brenda shed the filmy housecoat as she walked. It fluttered to the floor like a small bird falling from its nest. Despite the tough life she had led, her assets still seemed to be in place and about as tight as one would expect for a woman in what Hughes guessed to be her thirties, latter thirties. Hughes' eyes were transfixed on the side-to-side twitch as her backside seemed to set a rhythm like a metronome.

Brenda pulled a pair of toreador pants from a drawer and wiggled into them with the ease of a modern aircraft carrier passing through the Panama Canal. Bending at the waist the Twins swung about like two massive gongs that had been struck to send a message. She slid her feet into the elevated platform shoes and then pulled down a skimpy top, most likely a T-shirt that had been chopped and channeled for the purpose of maximizing minimum coverage. The two massive orbs hung pendulously beneath the cotton fabric but only the top half being concealed. Hughes had snapped more than a dozen picture with the trusty Minox by this time – its silent operation not giving away his level of distraction with the show taking place across the room as if he weren't there.

As Brenda stuck her face in front of the mirror she caught the sight of the last of Hughes' photographic efforts before she called him on his continuous perversion and lack of professionalism. Sheepishly, Hughes replaced the Minox in his pocket and then realized that next to his pocket he had a problem of a slightly different nature. Immediately, he threw his notebook over his lap. Fortunately, for Hughes it wasn't a big problem. Brenda looked at Hughes' correctional efforts and said, "pity."

Icons

"Come with me." As quickly as Brenda had moved from filmy housecoat to Toreador she had gathered up her things and was swinging the screen door open with a no-nonsense command to Hughes to follow her, immediately.

Strutting several strides ahead of the quintessential dweeb, Brenda set a pace for the Boulevard turning left from her Ivar digs and marching as if on parade toward some unspecified destination. She paused long enough in front of the CVS pharmacy to let the Twins have a look at the inventory of potential male partners that she might choose to draw on later. With each step taken in the tipsy platform heels and the Spandex toreador pants, the sprayed on appearance of the bright red pants seemed to say with each twitch from left to right, "Ass for Rent," "Ass for Rent," "Ass for Rent," but then one could also surmise Brenda would have altered the lettering in the flashing neon sign that was her butt to say "Good Times Here," "Good Times Here," "Good Times Here."

The discombobulated Hughes arrived at Vince's Video, "Best on the Boulevard," several strides behind his subject. She marched through the store as if it were her own living room and headed for a set of swinging red doors that permitted only adults. Brenda twisted back to look for the reluctant, bespectacled professor who was so conspicuously out of his element. "Come on," she snapped, "hurry up!"

Although he would not admit it and most likely didn't see it anyway, Hughes would not, could not acknowledge he had just entered a world of his peers. In his mind he had established a utopian universe in which he sounded like Einstein, looked like George Clooney, and sexually performed like the legendary John Hobes. He was an interesting mix of physical and intellectual capabilities, even if only in his imagination but the foundation was so concretely rooted there he was blind to reality.

Once in the adult section of Vince's Videos, Hughes' head swiveled from one degenerate to another. He could not trust such people. They were morally, socially and physically unclean; they were also intellectually depraved and on a plain so far beneath him that conversation would have been meaningless. His eyes moved from one customer to another. There was the thirtyish Black bulwark of a specimen. He had his sound system firmly affixed to his head; his feet moved fluidly as he perused each VHS and DVD jacket for the pictures of lurid sex acts being performed by actors and actresses all of whom seemed to have immigrated from a different galaxy, from a planet known only as *Endowment*.

There was also the slender man who stood as far into the corner of the darkened room as possible - his lady-like fingers picking through one row of porn after another much like a concert pianist picking his way across the keyboard in celebrated manner. Unlike the young Black male who

87

concentrated on each picture as if in study, the slender fellow in the corner moved through the plastic boxes quickly, his eyes more on the other customers than on his shopping needs. . . but then, perhaps his eyes *were* on his shopping needs.

The group in the store also included sundry men in their fifties and sixties, some most likely homeless others were most likely local residents of the seven hundred square foot stuccos that populated Hollywood. These men most likely didn't even own a video player; they got their jollies right in the store. There was also the quintessential example of a cross-dresser making his or her way about the store paying hardly any attention to the products – just the customers. And lastly, there was the bull dyke in her leather, chains and enough piercings to negate any possibility of every passing through an airport.

Once again the silence of the smut sanctuary was broken when Brenda snapped at Hughes who nervously dodged the dregs of society as if he were playing dodge ball. On order, he stepped to the back of the room to join Brenda.

As Hughes moved close enough to Brenda to anchor upon her as the only person in whom he felt safe, Brenda jerked a curtain to the side to yet another room, this for the "privileged" customers. Hughes had stepped into Brenda's world without understanding the threshold over which he had just crossed. The walls were covered, every square inch, with movie posters – not *Gone With the Wind* or *Saving Private Ryan*, but posters of Brenda's countless movies. There was the thirty-six by forty-eight inch paper tapestry of Two Guns Ablazin', starring Brenda; there was Twin Towers of Money and Honey also starring Brenda and many more. She walked down one aisle then another randomly pulling videos from the shelves and flashing them in the Hughes' face.

Like most everything else she had tried to communicate to the pseudo-academic, she showed her success, her place in life, her raison d'etre. Hughes saw T and A in abundance and in positions that caused his fragile condition to become tedious.

The Glory Days

"Let me tell you about the days on the set. . . those were the days." Brenda's voice trailed off as a cloud of nostalgia hovered within her cranium. They had left the video store once Brenda had believed she had made her point – that being that she had been the *Queen, Numero Uno*, the *Princess of Flesh* in a sea of flesh known as Hollywood. Hughes' level of distraction remained at the overload threshold. Such research was ideally suited to his prurient interests but ill-suited to his success as a legitimate researcher. He had let his libido become immersed in the pot of flesh rather than assessing the pot as a detached observer.

A crisp right cross delivered an opened-handed wake-up call across Hughes' cheek and sent him reeling, partly because he couldn't take the pain and partly the shock value that Brenda had hoped to deliver. "What the hell was that for?" He barked in wounded ego fashion.

"I thought this interview was so damn important to you and all you can do is to keep your beady little eyes focused off in space. Do you want to do this or not? This is

your last chance, little man. Screw with me one more time and Mr. Kung Fu from downstairs will break your ass in half and leave it with the night's trash." Brenda was riled and her metaphors were coming about as easy as her gait on her WalMart platforms heels .

Four fingers of glowing red highlights flashed on-and-off on the side of Hughes' face as he ripped back and forth through his notes to get organized. Again, sitting in the Ivar Palace, Hughes tried anew. "Tell me about the height of your film career." Hughes clicked the little black device to record and centered a pencil above his pad.

Something akin to calm seemed to settle in over the Hollywood area as Brenda began recounting the highlights of her life. Stillness seemed to pervade the otherwise noxious din of traffic noise outside. Brenda's body seemed to relax and the tension seemed to fade from her demeanor. "You don't know the sensation of countless assistants running about to take care of your every need or everyone, men and women alike, telling you how beautiful you are every waking hour of the day. To see men stare at my chest and actually drool, to see in their faces just how desperately they wanted me – that's a powerful set of feelings."

Brenda adjusted herself to the other side of the couch's errant spring and continued. "I'd be picked up in a stretch limousine and whisked away to a set or to a photo shoot someplace. Everyone would scramble to ride with me and always asking if they could have a peek. The more adventurous, the older men who put up the money for the films would ask more of me as we drove about L.A. asking that I do things to myself. I didn't mind. They were paying the freight and this was the business I was in. Besides, I always turned myself on at least as much as them."

Brenda....A Whimsical Look at a Fallen Star

The Vietnamese store owner below was apparently preparing dinner; fumes of charred animal flesh were wafting up the stairwell and immersing Brenda and Hughes in a cloud of grease-laden smoke. A smoke alarm erupted somewhere below Brenda's apartment and the little man could be seen running about in his rolled-up pants and sandals screaming incoherent profanities in a language completely alien to Hughes, somewhat familiar to Brenda. At the height of the confusion she stepped to the top of the stairs and shouted downward half dozen words in Vietnamese. Shortly thereafter the smoke alarm was terminated. "Now where were we? Oh yes. . . ."

"Are you aware that I made more than three hundred films? Feature-length films. . . . I also made countless loops, you know those things they run in the machines in the backs of porno shops. For a quarter you get to see two or three minutes of the loop. You have to keep feeding the kitty quickly so that the play is in sequence or if you allow it to recycle your next quarter will make it start from the beginning again. No one really likes those things but it is expected."

Brenda turned to the door as her friend Debbie arrived. They tried to slide past each other in the doorway and got locked together about chest high. Each looked down at the impediment and began to laugh and slowly eased their way free. "Hi. Come on in. The Professor Doctor and I are talking about the height of my film career. You can help fill in the gaps if I forget something." Debbie followed her olfactory senses into the tiny apartment. The air outside was oppressive and could turn a watermelon simply to water and then into a diffuse pink mist absorbed by the heat; on the inside, the air was mildly pungent given the absence of air conditioning and the ever present cloud given off by cooked animal flesh. Rumor had it that Ding Vinh cooked anything

92

he could catch, doused it with hot sauce and served it to his unwitting customers as amplitude to his liquor store sales.

"Sure baby," oozed Debbie as she made the transition from one environment to another. "Anything you say." Debbie sat down following Brenda. She pulled her feet up under her and pressed her torso against Brenda, looping her arm around Brenda's shoulder. Debbie had long wanted Brenda but never pushed the issue; they were friends first, last, and foremost and she was smart enough to know that an inappropriate or awkward overture could jeopardize that relationship. In fact, Debbie loved Brenda. She had made the awkward transition from men to women following a gang rape just a block from the apartment they now shared. She had been scarred more emotionally than physically.

Brenda responded to the closeness of her friend by twisting her head around and planting a kiss on Debbie's cheek. They smiled and then Brenda returned her attention to Hughes who was obviously waiting to see a girl-on-girl show evolve from the display of friendship between the two. Brenda's return to the topic was disappointing and could be measured by Hughes' facial expression which was as much like a barometer for sexual arousal.

"Okay, here we go again," Brenda so broke the moment of tension that existed for the professor. "I had posters decorating every adult theater in LA, a stack of glamour photos as deep as I am tall, and enough videos to fill this room - that, my little professor man, was success, spelled with a capital 'S'." Hughes scribbled in his note pad and looked up as the two ladies made eyes at each other. His thoughts were centered on the word success. He thought, *if I'm a success and have managed my achievements with all my clothes on and no one climbing all over my body while she*

claims to be a success. . . there must be a sliding scale for the definition of success.

King John

"Do you think, Sweetie, I should tell the Professor Doctor about the King?" Brenda's eyes twinkled at the anticipation of revealing one of her greatest moments. "Dare I mention his name?" Brenda giggled like a giddy school girl, her dimple never more prominent in a face that desperately wanted to smile and signal her enjoyment of life.

Brenda looked at the dubious professor and raised her arms, her hands clasped together. Slowly she inched her hands apart until they were what she thought to be a little more than a foot apart. "He was the king," she said almost in a tone of reverence.

Professor Hughes was beginning to find it difficult to sit comfortably; he fidgeted and twisted back and forth in his chair to conceal his level of anticipation. His notes became more and more obsequious with regard to the vixen across from him who verbally fawned over the mental image of a fallen star – a man who actually died a pitiful death from a grossly debilitating HiV infection - AIDS. For Hughes this was almost on a par basis with watching one of his dozens of pornographic videos – this, however, was in the flesh and he could envision actions that had taken place years before as if they were being performed in front of him at the moment. The lascivious nature of the monologue spilled from the ruby-colored lips of the former porno queen at an increasing pace. She too was getting caught up in the moment as the memories flooded through her mind like water released from the Hoover Dam. Her eyes closed momentarily, her body shuddered and her commentary stopped abruptly. Slowly she turned toward Debbie as her eyes opened and a huge smile enveloped her countenance. Debbie understood even if the troll across from them was clueless as to what had just taken place. Brenda had had many encounters for the camera, before the camera, after the camera and during her personal time as well. However, no one had ever wrung her bell like the infamous John Hobes. His physical presence demanded every ounce of spiritual commitment to the process; there was no faking, no ignoring, no blasé attitude about well, here's another one, let's get it done and get paid. On the contrary, Brenda had considered foregoing her pay just to be teamed with the penile giant on as many occasions as could be scheduled.

"If you haven't put two and two together yet professor, John Hobes was special. Not only did he fill a need, he filled everything else. . . he was nice. . . considerate. He treated me like a lady. So many of those cowboys just saddle up, ride for their eight seconds, and then dismount. They're really more like the rodeo clowns than anything. Actually, our many appearances together in "feature films" was what our fans got to see. In reality, he was over here almost every night." Brenda's eyes glassed over slightly, not that the professor noticed but a point not lost on the ever-faithful Debbie. "I was in love with him." The room fell silent. Even Hughes looked up from his doodles on the edge of his notebook where he had made several dozen illustrations of Brenda's primary assets.

"I thought that people in your profession treated their work as just that and didn't get involved with one another. Am I missing something here?" asked a more attentive interviewer.

"To my way of thinking, professor doctor, you have missed most everything. I don't really know why I'm pouring my heart out like this." Brenda choked back a sob that was about to engulf her demeanor but she remained firm and stared directly at the professor, at his perplexed expression.

"If you haven't figured it out yet, he was the first man who truly cared for me." Barely a whisper slipped past Brenda's lips as she tried to remain objective for the sake of the interview. "I had thought that Rocko had cared. I was wrong. He simply used me like so many others. But John. . . ." Brenda's voice trailed to a place somewhere over the horizon of reality. She was temporarily lost in a moment of splendiferous melancholy.

"Why did you think your John cared for you Brenda? What was so different that he wasn't just using you like everybody else but had found your number and stroked you to keep getting the goods?" Hughes lips perched to one side as a smirk settled on his face. He had seen through the remarkable John Holmes and was now in a position to get to the heart of a critical social contradiction that had become a personal crutch for Brenda. If he could make her see that Holmes had simply used her like all the rest of the men passing through the "meat grinder" he would have stripped away that last element of pseudo dignity upon which Brenda's self-esteem rested. Hughes would then be in a position to challenge Brenda at the

most fundamental level and understand what made the girls tick who worked in the porno industry.

"Damn you, you little man, you piece of dried up dog shit! How dare you play with my feelings as if they were yours to control. You don't know what went on between John and I, you don't know how he felt about me."

Debbie wrapped her arm around Brenda's shoulders and stared across the small space that separated the two women from the self-assured college professor. "Get your bony ass out of here right now," she screamed. Hughes swore later that at that moment he saw a protrusion of fangs emanating from Debbie's upper jaw and that her fingernails had instantaneously stretched two inches out like tiger claws.

"But. . . but I can't leave now. Don't you see, I'm on the verge of understanding what makes a whore like this tick?"

Debbie sprang from the couch landing her right knee in the professor's groin, her right hand sweeping through the air simultaneously in a downward arc. Her knuckles crunched into the bony structure of a face that needed serious reconstruction before Debbie began an all-out assault like a bare-knuckle boxer. The former kung fu instructor and VC soldier who now operated the liquor store below Brenda's apartment had heard the commotion and raced up the rickety stairs. He tore through the screen door just in time to pull Hughes from a death grip that Debbie was inflicting on the scrawny man's throat. The sinewy Asian grabbed Hughes by the belt and shirt collar and hurled him out the door and down the steps – Hughes landing in a rumpled pile and barely conscious. . . and without his notebook or tape recorder.

Recomposition

Debbie had caught up to the delirious Brenda as she had run down the street ranting in a delusional rancor. Debbie caught up to her friend just as Brenda had just agreed to sell herself to a down-and-out doper. The tattered skeleton of a man was so high he would have been physically incapable of consummating his "love contract." The seller in this business arrangement had prided herself in not resorting to selling *it* for more than three years – it had been her own Alcoholics Anonymous program of sorts. Now, however, thanks to the demeaning implications of Hughes' comments she stood at the threshold of defiling herself and thrusting her self-esteem back into the dark pit out of which she had fought diligently to climb.

Debbie dragged her wailing friend into the All American Burger on Sunset Boulevard as a refuge from the din of traffic and streets where Brenda had lived so much of her shattered life. The brightly lit restaurant seemed to be an attempt to create an eatery in the Hollywood area where tourists and locals could find some semblance of "American"

food. In that there are eighty-seven languages and dialects spoken in the Hollywood area many of the restaurants tended to be one form of cultural adaptation or another – with little appeal to the hog farmer from Iowa who has come to visit the haunts of his former icons like Clark Gable and Errol Flynn. The hog farmer was no more out of place in Hollywood than the southern belle from South Carolina who wanted to drive past the studios and walk the streets where Marilyn Monroe and Jayne Mansfield had walked.

All American Burger was a refuge of sorts after the hog farmer and the southern belle slowly came to realize how much Hollywood had degenerated since its glory days, how the restaurants were Thai, Chinese, Mongolian, Greek, Japanese, Mexican, Persian, and more.

Debbie and Brenda sat at a small booth toward the rear of the restaurant where Brenda's sobbing and ranting would be less malodorous to the other patrons. "Why did that little bastard have to come into my life and dredge up all the old devils and pain? Why couldn't he be smart enough to know when to stop or have any sensitivity for the nightmare that has been my sad life? Why?"

The restaurant was a flurry of activity, waitresses in their red, white and blue striped costumes darting from table-to-table and in-and-out of the kitchen as if they actually cared about getting an order correct and delivered to the table promptly. As Debbie watched the goings on before responding to Brenda it seemed as if all motion had abruptly shifted gears into a slow motion cycle. Debbie and Brenda were in real time while the rest of the restaurant seemed to almost stand still. *This is a sign*, Debbie thought. Her eyes switched back to the red, swollen face streaked by mascara streamers and smeared lipstick. "Brenda! Don't you see? This is a sign," Debbie exalted with great exuberance. Brenda

looked up from her table-bound gaze with no more sense of expression that the restaurant's front door held to its inner element.

Debbie reached across the table taking Brenda's face between her calloused palms and tried to wipe away the black streaks that had formed from Brenda's eyes to her chin. "Sweetie, you've just been given a second chance at life. Don't you see? This whole thing was meant to be. . . the miserable little bastard had been sent to you by some mysterious power that we'll never understand to cause you to refocus your life. You've bottomed out girl and this is the sign; this awakening has been through that degenerate and his little tape recorder. I see it all so clearly and so will you when you stop crying and forget big John. You've just been given a second chance at life, a chance to become a star once again. Your first career is history and you have lamented your fall from the limelight and stardom but you can now stand up and move forward. As they say, this is the first day of the rest of your life. Let's celebrate and talk about where you're headed. I can't wait to think about the celebrity that will embrace the renown of Brenda Disper.

Debbie's Game Plan

The following day was a mirrored reflection of the preceding day, and the one before, and the one before, and so on. The weather doesn't change a whole lot in LA. One day it will start to rain, lightly and without thunder or lightning, and the infrequent drizzle will end two months later. That was the winter. Other than that it was summer.

Today was winter, but not as a Chicagoan would recognize it. The crowds on the boulevard had thinned which meant the lunchtime swarm to the areas restaurants where ne'er a word of English could be understood and where the food floated above a shine of grease on the paper in which lunch was wrapped. Debbie burst through the unlocked, rattling screen door which had been the only protection between the sexual scavengers who preyed on the area's women and a recumbent Brenda who was splayed across the rumpled sheets. Brenda only slightly responded to the rattle and screech that would have stood most people's hair on end. "Brenda! Get up! WeI have to talk. Get up! Now! Come

on, get up!" Debbie began to tickle Brenda's feet; a condition she knew would get a response. Brenda hated it.

Brenda bounced around the bed like an armadillo turned on its back in the middle of a steamy Texas highway. Screaming hysterically, she pleaded with Debbie to cease fire. She would get up. However, in each intermission Brenda would flop back to the rumpled sheets like a sack of potatoes. She was caught up in the morbidity of dealing with the comments of the miserable little man who had taken her twice-cycled life and turned it upside down once again. She was miserable. Her level of depression was comparable to that when she was told by the Brazen Films, Ltd. that her services were no longer needed and when her idol John had died so unceremoniously.

Debbie had a plan, however, and she would not let the *drearies* unsettle her good idea.

Finally, in an act of desperation, Debbie splashed her glass of beer into the face of the sullen ex-princess of porn. Brenda bolted from the bed, her face dripping with beer and caught in a moment of complete shock and disarray. After a second of two when reality dawned upon the intemperate Brenda, she hissed a response to Debbie's challenge, "what the hell was that for?"

"I'm sorry sweetie, really I am. But you have to get up and you're in such a funk that I need to get your head realigned – get you out of the doldrums. I've got an idea. We need to talk but first you need to get up, get cleaned up and we'll take a walk. Then I will tell you my idea. You'll hate it. I guarantee." With that, Debbie donned a becoming smile for her closest of all friends, actually her only friend. She tugged on the nightshirt matted to Brenda's beer-drenched upper torso. As it slid off, Debbie momentarily froze as she stared at the body she wished she could possess but which she dared not consider as it would cost her the friendship she cherished. Brenda had been through the meat grinder of parental abuse and that of her father's friends, through the porno industry's films and loops, and turned a number of tricks on the street to sustain herself financially but her body, with some work, could once again be tight and supple, full and beautifully rounded where Hollywood expected roundness. Her face. . . it was tired but a clever makeup artist could overcome that. Some self-confidence and rest would provide for a resurrection – of sorts. "Come on. The world is waiting. . . for the re-emergence of Brenda."

Debbie dragged Brenda to the two foot by two foot shower stall, twisted the valves and pressed Brenda into the icy water. The howl that followed probably triggered car alarms for a three square block area. When Brenda had been cleansed of the beer and the sour mood in which she began the day, she tugged on a snug tank top – it was crucial to always give the Twins their role of prominence – some toreador pants and some flats. The two waved to the former kung fu instructor who said something like "I'll keep an eye on your apartment," but which was generally unintelligible. After an ample amount of walking Debbie jerked Brenda to a halt.

"Look," she said. "Up there." Debbie pointed across the intersection to a giant billboard that sat atop a low-rise office building from the forties or fifties. In dazzling color the billboard displayed a supine image of another sex icon. Just the woman's barely-clad body and her name, Angelique, were on the huge poster. Brenda looked at the image trying to comprehend why she had been dragged this far on foot to see a poster of a sex icon. . . whose bouffant hairstyle seemed out of date, whose face had obviously been worked by a plastic surgeon, and whose boobs must have required a communitywide campaign to recycle countless plastic soda

bottles. There she was – as fake as any human could be made to be, but there she was. "If a dumb looking broad like that whose boobs probably feel like bags of rocks can get this kind of notoriety and the money that follows, then a beautiful woman like you who is real and soft and fully human can do much better. Your problem, Brenda Disper, is exposure. You need exposure, before the right people, wearing the right clothes and makeup, speaking their language and. . . a new name. You know what Rock Hudson or Kirk Douglas, Dean Martin and John Wayne all had in common?" she asked of a bewildered Brenda.

"No, but I bet you're going to tell me." Brenda's demeanor began to lighten slightly as she could recognize that her friend was working hard to help her.

"Okay. John Wayne was Marion Morrison. Kirk Douglas was Danielovitch Demsky. Dean Martin was Dino Crocetti and Rock Hudson was Leroy Harold Scherer. As each of these guys started looking to make it big in the entertainment industry some Hollywood agent had their name changed to something cutesier that people would remember and created an image for all the movie-goers. We need to do the same for you."

"I'm sure you've got something in mind. Right?" Brenda's face was now perky and resplendent in a glow of happiness. Her friend was working her magic once again.

"You bet I do." Debbie had hardly waited for a response from Brenda before she continued. "Ready? You're Brenda. Not Brenda Disper. She's gone, history. Like our plastic friend up there, you are just Brenda. And I am your agent. Okay?" It was clear that Debbie had given the idea, no matter how simple it seemed, a great deal of thought. She was ready to commit all her energies to putting a new luster on a gem that had fallen from the table top and garnered some dust. She would put a new polish on this gem and sell it to the world in a whole new package. BRENDA, her Brenda.

Re-Emergence – The Basics

Resurrecting Brenda from the psychological mess she had become in recent years would be problem enough for anyone to tackle. However, to reshape the semblance of the former self into a top-shelf, marketable commodity in today's standards would be a Herculean task.

Debbie sat at Denny's restaurant until the late hours for several nights puzzling over a small pad of paper and guzzling coffee in prodigious quantities, taking only bathroom breaks from her self-appointed task. Her notes and task lists would not qualify for a Fortune 500 Power Point presentation but she understood the logic and the relative importance of each task. Adjacent to her lists she added a column to identify "source." To accomplish what she had set out to do would take considerable effort, effort equated to money – money that neither she nor Brenda had. Therefore the list had to incorporate a source for the services or a source that could be reliably tapped for the money.

Debbie hunched over the table and pressed her thoughts into the fiber of the paper snapping the lead repeatedly. The firmness with which she drove the pencil across the nibs of paper seemed to be an indicator of her resolve to see Brenda rise to stardom once again – this time in a legitimate arena.

Let's see, she thought. *We are going to need some clothes for Brenda, something not flashy or overtly sexy – something tasteful. Art down at Frederick's will have an idea who I can talk to, what stores to visit and where the best deals are. We need a classy hairstylist, a good makeup artist, some professional head shots, someone to build a portfolio for Brenda and, and, oh yes, someone to coach her on her grammar and etiquette.*

Debbie began to fidget, her body language demonstrating an increasing degree of discomfort as she reviewed her notes. *This is a tall order; how the hell am I going to pull all this together. I just have to, but how?* Debbie looked about the restaurant for an answer. If there had been one it had been lost in the din of waitresses shouting orders, "one BLT, hold the T, hold the mayo, hold the bread." That order even drew Debbie's attention from her focused activity. Of all the people up and moving about none came forward to Debbie's small table near the rear of the restaurant. No one seemed to offer their help or ideas on how to spring Brenda to the forefront of glamour ladies in Hollywood. *No,* she thought. *I'm going to have to do this myself unless. . . .*

An agent! Brenda needs an agent. He can choreograph all these jobs under one umbrella much better than I can do. I can act as his liaison or consultant between him and Brenda so that both parties work well together. We don't need another disaster like that little gnome from USC who nearly destroyed my precious Brenda.

Debbie slipped a single finger into a pocket that was compressed by the tightness of the Spandex outfit; she oozed a couple dollars out of the material and left it for her coffee. She needed to walk; she needed to think. A splash of chilled evening air might help bring some focus to her dilemma.

Debbie mumbled audibly as she crept along the star-inlaid sidewalk of Hollywood Boulevard, The Boulevard. *I have two issues to resolve: first, how do I get an agent to take on this job – it won't be easy. Second, what is it I'm offering him?* She thought some more as she turned an leaned across one of those metal vending machines that hold the Hollywood Star and various other T&A tabloids. This posture seemed inviting to more than one passerby. Had Debbie the mind to do so she could have made more than a hundred dollars without any solicitation needed. Debbie reached behind herself and slapped her rounded booty made taught by the slenderizing fabric. *Hey,* she thought, *I've still got it.* The up lift gave her renewed vigor to focus on her two questions.

By this time Debbie had reached Grauman's Chinese Theater. She ambled around aimlessly looking at the hand and foot prints of the biggest names Hollywood had created. They were true stars. They had earned their accolades over protracted careers and were not like the one night stands of today's Hollywood. Today some underfed teenie with blonde hair, no voice, not a single dance step, but unscrupulously loose morals and an articulate penchant for gaining the eye of the television camera became a "star" instantly. The more preposterous, the higher their star seemed to rise; the worse their public behavior, the faster their star rose.

Brenda is a package, Debbie thought. *She is a natural package. She is down to earth, sweet, not plastic inflated, she is a victim of the evils of our society. She had been taken advantage of and pulled into the sewer and without any guidance or help her life was taken from her. Hey, this is good. The news is filled every day with stories of people whose lives were screwed up by some oversexed relative, some slick-talking purveyors of filth pandering to a sex-hungry public. There is a true human interest story here besides she is natural, physically and morally. There's a lot to work with there – the Brenda package. Now, how do I pitch that to an agent? Hell, how do I find an agent, one from the right side of the tracks?*

Debbie was so struck with the obvious answer that she sat down immediately before she fell down. She plopped where she had stood; she had one of Clark Gable's hands under each of her cheeks, derriere, that is. "Ooh Mr. Clark, I wish we had known each other better. . . while you were alive I mean." Passersby smiled at the ribaldry as Debbie never really just spoke in social tones. Everyone became part of the audio landscape of a Debbie monologues when she was over the top with depression or a tyrannical outrage.

"Max! Max Stern. How much more obvious could it be? He's the man, polite, educated, well connected and, and he made a comment to me once when Brenda and I were serving drinks at that MGM party. Oh yes, he's got an interest in Brenda. He'll help her but I have to find a way to offer him the goodies without delivering. That's the link I have to see to it that gets broken from Brenda's psycho-social behavior pattern – a broken promise without any negative consequences. Rising from Mr. Clark's hands, Debbie was absolutely gleeful as a chorus of Japanese tourists proceeded to applaud and photograph every movement. "Jeez, did I just put together a good idea, or what?" she was heard to say as she meandered down the Boulevard.

Max Stern

There is no throne behind which there is not a clever, articulate string-puller capable of causing a desired outcome while remaining beyond the limelight. . . and scrutiny. Such were the credentials of Max Stern – Jewish, an attorney, reared in Brooklyn and came to Hollywood to manage the careers of some of those he represented in his legal practice. Before emigrating from the old country with his parents just ahead of Hitler's deadly overtures, the name had been Sternelovitch.

It had been in the sixties when he had shifted his focus from strictly legal issues to the coddling of a small group from Hollywood who operated in the rarefied environment of stardom. Such people seldom knew how much money they had, how to save, how to spend – some didn't even know their zip code. They moved from one day to the next by the guidance of their "handlers." Max was the handler's handler. He employed a cadre of subordinates who took most of the guff, the rebukes, the tantrums and self-inflicted abuse by drugs and alcohol. When such a celebrity passed a given threshold, however, Max got the call and he moved to the front lines. His expertise centered on defusing egos on the rant before the person or the issue drew media attention; when the call came too late, he managed the media.

Stern had managed the careers of some of Hollywood most articulate losers – people whose film or music careers had been catapulted to the ether but who were at a loss to wipe his or her own butt without instructions from a "handler." Stern had also dabbled at the other end of Hollywood's smorgasbord of talent – those who had no talent save for that which jiggled pendulously for public display and those who were willing to utilize any orifice to gain recognition their ego sought. He wined, dined, and had the most beautiful air-heads producers led to his door. He had them from the Mexican peninsula to the Dry Tortugas on his little "get-aways" from the public eye. Now he was being given a real treat it seemed. Someone had called and offered him a target he had relished a couple years earlier but which had been unattainable at the time. Brenda.

Stern thought he recognized the voice of the caller and easily remembered the landscape features of Brenda – mountains of softness, valleys of mystery and the suggestion of an all-expense paid safari through the wilds possessed by the former sex goddess, Brenda.

"What can I do for ya darlin?" Stern sat at his desk high in the north triangular tower at Century City, a futuristic development on LA's far Westside. His feet were crossed atop the glass table that served as his desk. In the notched "v" formed between his two feet he could see the heart of Hollywood to the right of the tassel on his Italian loafers. The bluish smoke of his Cuban contraband, as he referred to his cache of premium cigars, formed a cloud of a slightly different hue than the discoloration that permeated the skies hanging

over the city. All about the office were pictures of Stern in the embrace of one Hollywood icon or another. Such simple mementos were part of the aurora which one must be able to display as part of his due diligence. He knew the "in crowd" and they loved him, to wit, the carefully scribbled notes on the black-and-white glossies. Elsewhere in his capacious office one could see, as if on public display, the trappings of business success. If viewed from a more cynical perspective, all these trappings, the digs, the Italian loafers and the palatial estate in Holmby Hills were attributable to a lifestyle derived from being a leach. He fed like a common parasite on the success of others; his success was derived from the success of others. As their careers faded and no attempt to reinvigorate their malignancies would help, Stern simply dropped the dead weight and found a new source. He smelled such blood; he smelled such money potential when he thought of the sex goddess gone asunder but apparently with new life – and earning potential.

"Mr. Stern, I will admit to hardly knowing you but know quite well of you. I know what you're capable of if the stakes are high enough and the game is played right." Debbie continued nervously over the phone speaking as if her chance meeting with Stern at the studio's cocktail party had been as if she had been a strong young hopeful. In reality, she had simply served his drinks and canapés. She had worked diligently, however, to overhear as much of his conversations as possible as she darted about the room in her black-and-white uniform. Today was the day to make that effort pay off. "I represent Brenda. I believe you remember her. . . ." Debbie let the thought hang in the electronic air of the telephone as if a cloud perched in the sky. She was waiting, albeit briefly, for a mental image of Debbie to run its course from his ear, to his groin and back to his brain. "Bottom line,

I want to transfer the rights of representation from myself to you."

Max Stern eased his feet from the glass table and rocked forward to rest his elbows on the table. "And for this you want a sizeable commission I trust."

"Actually. . . no I don't. There is another fee that you will need to pay." Stern's level of apprehension grew with each new verbal challenge by the young woman whose face he could not quite place mentally. He worked his mind through his mental database as she spoke: chest, face, chest, face, chest, face and so. He couldn't quite put a face with the chests he remembered from the studio party but he continued to listen. He was intrigued by the audacity of the challenge of a "fee" he would have to pay to gain access (whatever that might mean or where it might lead) to the infamous Brenda.

"Okay, I bite. What do you want?" asked the *follicly-challenged* balding ex-New Yorker.

Debbie then grabbed her sword and thrust it into the imagination and wallet of the man at the other end of the line. "Brenda has wonderful assets, huge potential. . . but she also has some rough edges. They're not her fault. She had a pretty sad childhood which led her to the venue from which you know of her. If you want to take on this hot property you must commit to a complete make-over of my friend Brenda. She needs clothes, she needs a hair and makeup artist to get the right headlines on her front page and she needs some coaching with regard to etiquette and language skills. Anything else you want to add like singing or dancing would be money you'd be throwing out with a clear expectation of an even larger return on your investment." Debbie concluded her pitch and let some white space pervade the air between the two telephones.

Finally, Stern spoke. "That's a pretty tall order young lady. What's in it for me?" An overwhelming smile settled on his face with that question but with the hope that the smile didn't show through the phone lines.

"Well, darling, you get Brenda of course. Whatever relationship the two of you mutually develop beyond a purely professional decorum is between the two of you now, isn't it?" Debbie teased out the response to the 'what's in it for me' question.

Stern began to chew vigorously on the stump of the cigar. A chemical reaction had apparently begun somewhere within selected organs and his discomfort was beginning to remonstrate throughout his body. "Yeah, that would do it, wouldn't it?" The words sort of dribbled out of his mouth not as a question, not even as a declarative but more as a phallic thought that slipped beyond his subconscious and over his lips like a small belch following a gulf of champagne.

"Then we have a deal?" Debbie began to tingle from the opportunity to get far enough to actually raise that question without it being rhetorical.

"Yeah. Yeah, er I mean yes we do young woman. What did you say your name is? I've being trying to place your voice and I'm not quite there.

Reluctantly Debbie oozed a response to Stern hoping that she could remain just out of sight, out of the limelight and beyond recognition.

The "Clean-Up" Crew

Brenda was so caught up in the flurry of activity that now surrounded her life she was lost for words – a condition that seldom characterized her demeanor. Debbie's gamble had paid off and after only a few days she had a call back to have Brenda ready to relocate to a place to live on the edge of the hills in Hollywood but within clear eye sight of the *Hollywood* sign – the sign that once had said Hollywoodland erected by a developer to promote his housing project in the hills above Hollywood.

The new "digs" were a dramatic improvement over the liquor store loft just off the boulevard. This small two-bedroom bungalow was the first place that Brenda had lived that wasn't an apartment. . . or an alley. It even had room for Debbie – a consideration not lost on the best friend who had quietly orchestrated the conditions for Brenda. The walls were conveyed in a Tope, the furniture was a mixed assortment of styles but all in good condition, the kitchen had appliances, even a dishwasher. But best of all it had windows and they looked out across the coastal plain that was the heart of Hollywood and Los Angeles and all the high-rise concrete and steel of downtown. On a clear evening one could see all

the way to Long Beach and with the aid of binoculars provided once by Stern it was possible to see Catalina Island.

Now the cute little bungalow that had one foot anchored into the hillside and the three opposing corners of the house propped with struts was abuzz with activity. Brenda sat in the center of the room while two young men bounced around her kitchen chair like the fairies who accompanied Peter Pan. Their feet seldom actually hit the floor as they sashayed about speaking to each other in a lilt that was dramatized by gesticulations of their hands and arms. They did, however, know their craft. Like alchemists of old, the two young men, Eric and Robin, sculpted a new look that spoke elegance and glamour. Their skills had been honed in the salons of Beverly Hills where work conditions could not be more extreme and they had each succeeded and risen to the top of their unique profession. Now Brenda had become the latest beneficiary of their skills and of the praise they continued to heap upon her. This was like a salve for her ego. All the while, Brenda smiled a deeply affectionate glow toward the individual across the room that had made this possible.

Once the duo of Eric and Robin had performed their magic, a new entourage was ushered in by a man who served in the capacity of concierge. This group of artisans worked on the face, eyes, teeth, fingernails, toenails and exposed skin. Working singularly and sometimes in tandem the group took the raw iron ore and turned it into a shiny Maserati. The metamorphosis was nearly complete. It had taken a full day as well as some extra time for each individual to explain how Brenda was to maintain the appearance they had created. Before Brenda and Debbie could think about dinner there was one more compulsory visit – the "teacher."

Rudolph, Rudi for short, was a grammarian, a diction coach. His visit today was simply to make an initial assessment of the scale of the problem he would be facing. He departed with something akin to a smile on his face as it now seemed that his benefactor, one Max Stern, had apparently over-dramatized the need for improvement to Brenda's speech patterns, pronunciation, word selection, and general enhancement of vocabulary. He had left Brenda with the thought, however, that numerous words would have to be omitted from her lexicon, most of these contained no more than four letters but there were also some hyphenated words and a couple longer ones that had to be dropped as well.

Debbie watched Brenda's new face as the two wolfed down a shared box of macaroni and cheese and a couple previously frozen hamburger patties, the combo of which was washed down with a Bud Light. It occurred to Debbie that they also needed some cash if her grand plan was to be fulfilled. It was magnificent that Stern had accommodated the make-over and was footing the bill for the small house but they needed cash. They needed to eat properly; Brenda needed to eat properly if her transformation was to have a foundation. She needed to appreciate the finer things, to know what to ask for, what tastes worked well together – in short she needed a quick dose of class. That would take cash and she didn't think that Stern represented a bottomless well to which they could run continually for anything they wanted or needed. On the other hand she had conceded direct managerial control over the property known simply as *Brenda* to Max Stern so she didn't have the latitude to negotiate deals for Brenda. *The* deal had already been made and they were reaping the benefits.

For his part of the arrangement, Max Stern had already written off the cost of the little bungalow. That had been part of a settlement between he and another client, the

arrangements between the two parties having gone *South*. As for the beauticians and hairstylists they bore no direct bottom line cost; they were borrowed from other clients who paid a flat fee for their services but whose services were under the direct contractual control of Stern.

Stern sat at his desk late in the evening. His staff had departed and he enjoyed the company of one Frenchman and one Cuban at this hour – his drink and his cigar. He dipped the business end of his Cuban into the substance that was his Frenchman, and voilà he had a wonderful cigar with a Cognac teaser. These were ultimately his best friends and whose company he kept regularly. Stern puffed away as he stared first at one image then another. He had convinced Debbie that he couldn't fix the problem if he didn't know to what degree it was broken so he managed to take dozens of Polaroids of Brenda: dressed, semi-dressed and tantalizing and completely nude in a variety of provocative poses. His appetite had been whetted and he was thinking main course. He had kept his part of the bargain and now was the time to reap the rewards. Oh yes, there would be a continuing level of support and the need to push the image forward but it was payback time nonetheless. Stern knew full well that pushing Brenda's image to magazine covers, billboards, and possibly even film would benefit his ego even more than it would fulfill Brenda's sense of destiny. That didn't matter. Being seen publicly with the best body to grace Hollywood since the sixties and bedding this chick on a regular basis was going to be worth the price. There had formed a truly symbiotic relationship between the two: each had what the other needed to be fulfilled and they would draw handily upon each other to satisfy their respective needs.

The Professor

Oblivion! I have managed to re-write the definition of the term. Oblivion. Shit. All this is traceable to that worthless little tart Brenda. She was never anything, she isn't anything, and she will never amount to anything. Yet, here I am, at the top of my profession, an academic and intellectual and look what that little tart has done to me. To make it worse, I've shelled out hundreds of dollars. . . that I could have kept for myself. Hughes' mind was cluttered with thoughts of chagrin, despair, and volatility toward the persona of Brenda – whose last name he had never recorded. He marched about his small ranch style fifties house in eastern Pasadena in his shoes and socks and nothing else. He had forgotten that he was changing clothes when he was once again overcome with an anxiety attack and his mind had spun off into the far reaches of space trying to reconcile his dilemma.

The ramshackle clutter that typified Hughes' small house had been taken to a new level following the dissolution of his agreement with Brenda to serve as the subject of his funded research. Tripping and swearing, the malcontent made his way through the area that seemingly had been a battleground between the god of sloth and the god of reason Hughes arrived at the icebox (today, a small refrigerator but not to be confused with the styles and models demonstrated by the lithesome models on television). Inside he reached for the milk, flipped the self-sealing spout and chugged down a couple mouthfuls before jerking away from the carton as if it had attacked him. As quickly as he could move he spat out the foul-tasting liquid, some of it actually hitting the sink, most hitting the counter, the window, the floor and other unintended targets. Snapping his glasses over his beaklike nose, he read the "use by" date only to find that that date had passed by more than a month. In disgust, he hurled the carton into the sink and paraded his scrawny, naked body into the bathroom. When he reached down to undo his pants to relieve himself he realized that there was no zipper, as there were no pants to unzip. Hmmm, he thought without any actual point of focus.

Shuffling through the piles of neglect and disuse, Hughes found some clothes into which he slid irrespective of the reality that none of them would have ever been intended to go together. He sat at his laptop and waited for an answer to his dilemma to appear on the screen. Occasionally he would tap the Enter key as if that would inaugurate a response but it had performed no better than the Escape key, or the spacebar. In utter frustration Hughes drew down on a bottle of wine that had sat dormant and uncorked for the past few days and in the bottle he found the answer. He would make up the balance of the interviews himself as if they had actually been conducted. In other words, he would cheat. He would demonstrate to the faculty and to Steingrit's Committee at USC that his intellect was truly superior. And for those of limited scope and performance at the federal funding agency who couldn't see past the end of their busy noses, he would show them as well. The downside was that he would never be able to tell them

just how much smarter he was to drive home his point of superiority.

Tomorrow morning, I'll get started on this after grinding out a couple more lectures for next fall's freshman class. Tonight, guess I'll pick up a few things and get the deck cleared for action tomorrow. How exciting. . . .

This time when Hughes hit the Enter key, pure intellect flowed as if from the pen of James Joyce or another of the intellectual masters. The hours turned into days but the days turned into a voluminous document that, even though disjointed and replete with syntax errors, accounted for the life of a young woman drawn to the sex industry and what had become of her once she had proved too old and too "worn" to continue to attract the trench coat types in the Pussycat theaters of America.

When completed, the two hundred page report that would garner Hughes the balance of his research fee from the government held an Executive Summary that when synopsized said:

> Brenda, whose last name is being withheld as a matter of propriety, is the product of a broken home in which the father was abusive and an alcoholic and a mother who whored more for pleasure than for the money.
>
> Brenda naturally fell into a comparable pattern of lifestyles, slid in and out of drugs and ended up in the pornographic industry where, when made up for the camera held a certain exotic appeal. Her career, however,

was cut short as her looks began to fade and her box office appeal waned.

Ultimately, Brenda, unable to cope with the loss of recognition and the adoration of fans for whom such depravity holds appeal, committed suicide shortly after the conclusion of the interviews that have produced this study. While the author of this research was in attendance at the pauper's funeral for the young woman, no others from what had once been characterized as millions of fans bothered to attend.

Brenda is gone. Brenda is forgotten. She met an ignominious end to a meaningless life.

The report then trailed off into a protracted harangue of dribble that only a classic bureaucrat could comprehend and appreciate. Not appreciated was the need to read through the grayed grease stains that had soaked through the bottom of his anchovy and sausage pizza and a few withering marks left behind by perspiration from the glass of beer. The pizza and beer were as integral to the completion of the manuscript as the cheap grade of paper onto which it was printed. Why waste his grant money on a polished image when any self-respecting academician could clearly see the brilliance of his work no matter what the nature of the stains left behind by his slovenly habits. This ritualistic document which served to grab "free" money could clearly serve as a coaster – *no problemo*.

Strung Along

Brenda's new career, a perfect example of the term "Phoenix," had taken on a life of its own and sprouted wings as if it had risen from the ashes. There were the constant hair and facial appointments, some rudimentary acting classes, voice lessons, and a rigorous regimen of diction coaching. Debbie had been enlisted as a co-beneficiary of Max Stern's beneficence to see to it that Brenda read the newspaper every day and other current periodicals to the extent possible. Brenda was being brought from the Dark Ages into the Age of Enlightenment through a crash course to make her a saleable commodity and worthy of the attention of Max Stern. . . and his ego.

The changes were dramatic. Other than the voluminous tank top-teasing chest, Brenda was hardly the same person. The outer shell had undergone a metamorphosis, the changes to poise, charm, and knowledge were no less dramatic. In the space of just a couple months, Brenda had re-invented herself with the aid of Max Stern's money and the technical skills of a small cadre of worker bees.

Debbie looked each day at the new Brenda and her love slowly turned to worry and then to an abiding concern. Would the new Brenda be too beautiful, too accomplished, too sophisticated to continue to countenance the likes of the former street-hooker Debbie? There were no telltale signs and Debbie felt she could not force the issue. That would only brand her as a paranoid delusional – a new term that Brenda had picked up (the trick would be for Brenda to use the term correctly). To compensate for the degree of change that she was seeing, Debbie began partaking of the Max Stern benefits as well rather than sit idly and watch each session held for her friend. Max was not picking up on the subtle differences reported back by the beauticians and others that Debbie had begun her own transformation.

In the evenings the two girls would sit on the bed, sliding in and out of American Idol and The OC to compare notes about the day. Brenda had not paid a lot of attention to the reality that Debbie had begun utilizing the services of all of Max's little army of makeover artists but on this night a little light went on in the otherwise vacuous head of Brenda. "My God, Debbie, you're beautiful. I hadn't been paying much attention lately, I know, as I have to keep up with Max's requirements to learn new words, pronounce them correctly, read about the current events and so on. But girl, you've been a changin' yourself. I like what I see Debbie. You're beautiful."

Debbie blushed. It was the first outward sign of affection between the two since Debbie had enlisted the help of Max. Brenda had been right. She had been so consumed with the minutiae of preparing herself for something big but undefined that she had been losing touch with her one basis of reality – Debbie. "You aren't too bad to look at yourself, girl." Debbie dropped her face somewhat to avoid revealing any more of her inner being than she had already done.

Brenda was under enough stress without Debbie further complicating her friend's life.

Debbie needed a new strategy. She could see this as she sat staring at the side of Brenda's face and wistfully let her eyes roam the balance of the playground where she hoped one day to enjoy herself. *I need to twist this all a little so that it is me who wins this horse race in the end and not Max.*

The two slid into their respective beds amid a melodious strain of classical music, another of Max's requirements, wafted through the still hillside air above Hollywood. Max had insisted that Motown and the Beach Boys be a thing of the past if Brenda was to develop into a new image as she had said she wanted.

A rapping at the front door broke the spell that preceded sleep and encroached on the happiness that each girl felt in her heart. They each knew the knock. Who other than Max would knock on their door at this hour? It was his time to begin to collect on his investment. Max had visited with his two close friends throughout the evening as a way to ameliorate his mood after four hours of dealing with one of his more ostentatious dilettantes – cognac and cigars had accompanied him on his path to arousal.

"I'll get it, you stay in bed," came the advice from Debbie. Brenda sat up with a look of consternation addressing her friend.

The words from across the threshold came out with more than a slight slur, "I want Brenda. . . and I want you to get lost, baby." Debbie had to put it on the line right here and now if she were ever able to realize her own dream of her and Brenda together.

"Hi Max, uh, I mean Mr. Stern. What is it you want?"

"You know what I want. You have strung me along for months now and I have yet to get Brenda where I want her. Using his hands he created a visual image of where his mind had led him to this point.

Debbie had formulated a new plan in recent weeks. Her own makeover had been part of that strategy and now seemed to be the time to put the plan in place, regardless of the hour of the night or the fact that she was reacting rather than taking the lead.

"Max. . . Brenda can't see you this evening. It's a bad time for her if you follow my meaning." Max looked dully at Debbie hearing only a negative response and not able to put two and two together. "Max, Brenda is in the bathroom. She's been there on and off all evening. She's in her period and it is a particularly bad one. Are you getting the picture there, Max?"

"Oh yeah. . . but I want her immediately when all this bullshit ends. Do you hear me?" Max pointed his finger directly down at Debbie who stood before him wearing only the top to a button-up pair of pajamas. His finger only a couple of inches from her chest, Debbie decided that now was the time. Looking down at his finger Debbie reached up, took Max's hand and helped him undo each of the buttons, spread the pajama top wide open and then guided his hand around one of her ample breasts.

"I think, Max, you've been missing the obvious and it's time that you be paid for all of your thoughtful help. When I show you that I taught Brenda everything she knows I think you will see that you're going to be happier working

with the original and not the copy." The words nearly choked in her throat but there had to be a price, there always was. Debbie pressed herself up against Max and let her hands begin an age-old process that would be followed by using everything she had to completely knock Max off guard and redirect his energies in her direction and away from Brenda.

Oh, Brenda, sweetheart, if you only knew the price I'm paying so that I can have you later. Oh Brenda.

The preliminaries had been finished quickly as is standard protocol for drunks. The main event had begun and Debbie was getting slammed once again like a common whore. Tears rolled down her cheeks in a profusion of guilt and anguish.

Debbie's Ruse

Debbie didn't need acting classes like her close friend. She enveloped Max's ego much the way a chicken's egg envelopes the yolk. He was caught in the web she had spun as she turned the age-old profession into profusion of encounters that would have been Max's version of an LSD trip. Debbie had played him like a Stradivarius in the hands of Yo-Yo Ma. Her proof was demonstrable in the ever decreasing number of times that he indicated an interest in Brenda and in the gifts that seemed to mystically appear at the small house. Plan 2 had been working like a charm; Brenda could see what was happening and chose to remain mute for the time being. Max, on the other hand, understood nothing except that he kept getting his pipes cleaned in dynamic fashion. He was a happy man and could be *milked* further.

Debbie never lost sight of her goal. The constant inflow of baubles from Max was not her goal. The prospect of a continued, long-lasting relationship with the master of schmooze was not her goal. Brenda was her goal. Brenda had to be free of Max's control and she had to be free of it as well. But there was still more amplitude to be added to Brenda's

new life and image. Debbie had to see that process through until it was able to feed on itself and not draw from the resources of Max Stern. He had been good to Brenda, hell, he had been good to Debbie but he was a tool, if not a fool. He was getting paid back in a manner befitting his interests – he could have no complaints.

In her passion for Brenda, Debbie had to unfold a new element of her grand plan. She had diverted Max's attention from Brenda so as to keep her *pure* and unassailable by the master Hollywood player. Now she had to get him off of herself as well while still using his talents and money to get Brenda to the top of the heap once again, but legitimately this time. Debbie had winnowed a number of secrets from the master puppeteer of Hollywood's brightest and biggest that could be used to leverage her final thrust, so to speak.

Brenda had just been summoned for an audition – an accommodation to Max by an ever-grateful producer. Such men traded favors back and forth like chips across the top of a poker table. The script was entitled The Demure Goddess and read as if it had been scripted around the background and presence of Brenda. She giggled and bubbled all through the day tripping over one thing and then the next as her focus was sitting astride a lightly twinkling star somewhere far into the heavens. Debbie beamed with happiness as she had orchestrated the entire scenario as if she had scripted it, but she said little. She was too happy for Brenda to distract her from the spell that had been cast around the budding actress.

There was a knock at the door. The two girls looked at each other – the silence between knocks was deafening. The air seemed to be choking and the level of discomfiture had risen to a disquieting level. Max had not called on Brenda now for quite some time and his arrangements with Debbie

had all been accommodated away from the little hillside cottage. But now. . . there it was again.

Debbie rose from the table where the two were sharing a bottle of wine. Debbie tried to keep pace with the shooting star sitting beside her. She was as happy for Brenda as if she had been called in for the audition herself. Only one thing could be better at this moment, well, two actually. First, that the knock at the door not be Max Stern and second, that she be allowed to have Brenda for herself.

Knock. Knock. Again the sound at the door, it was less temperate this time. Debbie rushed to swing open the door with a story that she was conjuring as she moved. "Are you Debbie?" asked the delivery driver.

"Yes, why?" came the meek retort.

"Then this is for you." The brightly clad delivery agent handed over a small envelope and a bouquet of roses. "Have a nice day, mam." He turned and was gone before a question for him could form on Debbie's gaping lips.

"My dearest Debbie: the fact that you have to read this note rather than hear the message from me directly proves that I could not bear to see your face in grievous disappointment and that I am basically a coward. As it turns out, I have met someone, the right one, the final one and must terminate our delicious tryst. In point of fact, I don't even know your last name as I think about it. I will not go back on our arrangement to see to Brenda's career. It looks like an excellent opportunity is on the immediate horizon after which she, nor you, will need my help. I hope Brenda has some sense of what a good friend she has in you. I wonder if she will

ever know how you interceded to avoid her paying for my services. Very best wishes, Max."

The Bean Counters

"Mark, unless I'm going crazy, this girl in the ads for next week's movie premier is the same girl that I've been reading about in the Study Report by Professor Hughes at USC. It deals with how to re-integrate a person from the porno film industry back into mainstream society. The report says that the subject of the study could not cope with the level of rejection and soon after the interviews were completed she committed suicide." The thirtyish technocrat buried in a cubicle on a floor of cubicles in a building of cubicles spoke to his friend with an air of doubt circling about him like a buzzard over road kill.

"So where's the issue?" responded the next thrityish technocrat in the adjoining cubicle. Both Ivy Leaguers in their crisp shirts, club ties, sleeves rolled up, completing their "in" look with Dockers and casual loafers. They had been stamped out of a mold that produced people who were comfortable in cubicles but with an eye toward upward mobility to some illusory sacrosanct supervisory level.

Mark's cohort, Steven Chernigin, scratched at the intermittent facial hair placement that he lovingly referred to as a beard. "Well, the footnotes identify the subject as Brenda . . . no last name, just Brenda. The View Section of the <u>Post</u> points to an interesting film that will debut at Grauman's Chinese theater in Hollywood. The best part is an in-depth critique of the performance of the woman playing the female lead – her name is Brenda. It's the same woman. If she's dead, how is it she's still giving interviews?" A perplexed Chernigin turned to his friend asking the rhetorical question with both knowing the answer simultaneously.

"Quick!" called the friend over the eye-level partition. "Call disbursement and stop the payment you said you had authorized last week. At the pace they move they would not have sent it out yet. You've got to remember. . . we're the federal government. No need to do today what we can put off until tomorrow just so long as we can create a paper trail to protect our jobs and create the illusion of progress. Quick! Call Dorothy down on four."

Steven Chernigin swung into action the way that only the well-oiled federal machinery can do – when they're about to screw over someone or prevent someone from screwing over them.

The chatter level from the sea of cubicles seemed to slide into the what's-going-on mode. The elevated pitch of the young Princetonian had alerted his cohorts and the other cubicle residents that something was awry. Had one of their own just signed his own 1219 form effectively sending him to some remote office destined to governmental oblivion? Or had one of their own caught some grantee in the act parsing funds from their coffers illegally. If so, they could now all dance around the tribal fire as they toasted the poor SOB's cajones while they all chanted much like the animals in the

Orwelian Animal Farm: Federal bureaucrats good; Grantees bad! The theme they all hummed at different incantations and varying melodies doubtless held the same belief system if not quite the same lyrics - *(sung to the tune of America the Beautiful following twenty rapid shots of Jack Daniels):*

The Beasts Beyond the Beltway

Oh ye who seeketh our help,
Oh ye who mistakenly believe,
Oh ye who wanteth some,
Of the tax dollars you think are yours,
Ye shall geteth none and beg for more.

Remember now,
Remember forever,
Your money is ours,
You are but sheep.

We will do as we want,
We'll take your money,
We'll sacrifice your lives,
Your's is not to complain.

Remember now,
Remember forever,
We are the feds,
We do as we want,
We promise it all,
We deliver none,
We are the Feds,
We deliver none.

Before you are given to believe that the federal theme song is lyrically unbalanced, keep in mind that they can do as they want more than any others. Their little theme is cast to the melody of We are the Champions by Queen and even if not heard audibly, one knows upon entry to the federal compound of departments, bureaus, and societies the theme is still in their heads nonetheless.

Steven Chernigin knows he's got his. For a moment he had almost lost the game, giving money to a cheater outside the Beltway. Now he had claimed his right of passage and before the night fell he would stand proudly atop the chest of some poor slob who tried to cheat the system and get money out of Washington.

The Committee

Dr. Steingrit sat at his desk at the MLK building near the center of the USC campus. The squeak, squeak of his swivel rocker was a signal that he was bouncing in his chair like a small child on a new tricycle. Steingrit was ecstatic and gushed superlatives in behalf of Dr. Malcolm Hughes. Even Dr. Helen Brighthurst, shot down the hall to see what tumultuous event had triggered the kind of reaction she could hear from so far. It was not like Steingrit, the disciplinarian of bureaucratic virtue, to so thoroughly enjoy a moment so unencumbered. Something was afoot.

The paltry appearance of the small Gestapo Headquarters, i.e., the Office of the University Chancellor, Academic Qualifications Review Panel – Chairman, had taken on an instant luster. The air filled Steingrit's lungs to capacity with a sweet and fresh feeling. Even the normally bothersome students seemed somehow courteous and polite, at least for a brief period of exhilaration. A spontaneous eruption had accompanied Steingrit's reading of the letter from the U.S. Department of Education regarding Hughes' final project report. dealing with the *hooker in the wood*, or put more

politically correct, a condition rarely utilized by Steingrit, Ms. Brenda from Hollywood.

Steingrit read it again, "It is the opinion of this office that Professor Hughes falsified his findings in the report regarding his research subject.. Reportedly she had taken her own life prior to the summation of Hughes' report. Evidence to the contrary points to a very vital young woman who not only rebounded from the perils of her earlier lifestyle but she has emerged to a greater capacity than the previous level reported during her earlier film days." Steingrit was once again buoyed.

"Yahoooooo! I got that silly little son of a bitch. Finally, I got 'im." Steingrit started down the hallway hung with countless bulletin boards announcing educational opportunities at various universities around the world. It was class-change time and a burst of students erupted from a dozen doorways along the corridor. Most looked like homeless vagrants, all starting conversations on their cell phones, each with an ear plug to his or her MP3 player and all dragging along as if they were muscle deficient and devoid of facial expression. Steingrit was on his way to the adjacent building where he would find the intellectual deficit who headed the Psychology Department. He would finally exact his pound of flesh from the goofy-looking little man whose ego dwarfed his physical and intellectual reality. However, as Steingrit was bumped by a student large enough to require his moving through the doorway sideway, number seventy-eight on Saturday afternoons in the Fall each year, Steingrit was nudged to thought: *better to wait and not waste this moment. I'll see Hughes when I have my ducks all in order*, he thought.

Steingrit proceeded to convene an emergency session of his Professional Ethics Committee and without any dissenting votes had Hughes censured, managed a concurrence

on the appropriateness of Hughes repaying all funds he had expended, and finally had his tenure rescinded. This final action was tantamount to giving Steingrit the authority to have a paper drawn up for the university president summarily firing Hughes.

In the course of just a couple days Steingrit had realized a plan that he had hoped to employ more than twice as many years earlier. Hughes had always been just a hair beyond the reach of his short-fingered, swarthy hands. Now, on the other hand, he was firmly within the grasp of the man who looked more like a building framer than an academic.

"Thank you for joining me, Malcolm. I thought lunch at the 'U" Club might be a pleasant change."

Hughes' natural tendency toward paranoia, an interesting condition for an individual employed in his capacity, cautioned him to question why Steingrit would embrace his presence for a luncheon for the first time since his arrival on campus seven years ago. "Yes. Yes, it is nice, but I must ask Steingrit. . . this seems to be without precedent, just why am I so graced after all this time?"

"Well it's your report, Malcolm. You should know that."

Hughes ego sprang from deep within its hiding place among the defused neurons in his cranium. Then he understood. Steingrit had gotten feedback regarding his superior work on the report related to Brenda entitled, *Issues Related to the Recovery and Future of a Former Pornographic Industry Celebrity to Mainstream Back into Society.* Hughes regretted the cumbersome title to his research; he would have preferred something more akin to a conventional book title – a consideration that he was beginning to explore with several of

the key publishing houses in Manhattan. A typical research project, however, nearly conveyed the executive summary in the title.

Bolstered by the knowledge that the excellence of his work had finally turned Steingrit in his direction, Hughes sat erectly in his chair as he awaited the accolades to be announced. He was already chair of the department – a condition actually brought about by the accidental death of the previous chair-holder. Therefore, what might it be, he wondered as he worked diligently to minimize the smile that was creeping across his face. A long-term sabbatical, that's it. They're going to give me what is effectively a long-term paid vacation during which I can conduct whatever research I choose and then return to teaching later. As the thought moved from conjecture to knowledge, Hughes was less able to repress the smile. He bubbled at the table while all those around were merely chewing and drinking, intermixed with what was surely inconsequential conversation. His smile had finally cued Steingrit to the point that he was prepared to share with Hughes the acknowledgement of excellence he knew he deserved after the painful process of interviewing that disgusting little whore.

"Hughes." Steingrit paused and wiped his lips with the cloth napkin. "Hughes, you're fired. I want your office cleaned out, under supervision of course, by tomorrow morning and you off this campus. Here. . . " Steingrit passed a copy of the feds' letter to Hughes. "Read this. The feds have exacted a series of conditions which you must meet in addition to those which we require. You're done Hughes. Finally." Steingrit took the napkin, folded it with his stubby fingers and placed it adjacent to his plate of uneaten food. "And by the way, Hughes, you can pick up the check for this meal."

The head of the university Gestapo laughed aloud as he laced his way between tables heading for the exit.

The Wanderer

A life without anything to reinforce his ego had turned Malcolm Hughes into a wandering soul devoid of spirit and purpose. His dismissal two months earlier had effectively sealed his academic career, particularly when considering that falsification of a federally-funded report was the genesis of his exile.

Hughes sat in his overstuffed chair facing the television, a plethora of men's magazine discarded about the floor; he was unable to bring into focus a course of action that would restore a means of livelihood and dignity to his life. The disarray of his small house, clothes scattered as if a police raid had been conducted, unwashed dishes standing about every flat surface in the kitchen, the dim lighting all served to mirror the image of the man himself. A splotchy beard had long since formed on his bony face with patches of hair growing at differing rates. His clothes hung about his emaciated figure, the fly on his pants undone, stains decorating the front of his trousers, his shirt partially buttoned and askew. Hughes had not brushed his teeth in some

unknown number of days. His diet had been meager and consisted of eating the catsup and mustard and other condiments as the food had long since been exploited. He ate only when so nauseated that something in his digestive system was obligatory.

Adding to his woes, the bank had posted a foreclosure notice to his front door for non-payment, his credit cards revoked for non-payment, and his bank account overdrawn. One of the conditions exacted upon Hughes by the Department of Education had been the repayment of all funds he had expended in the conduct of his research since that research had been falsified and his credibility zeroed out.

Hughes had to be out of the house before six that evening but had nowhere to go, no one with whom to stay, no one to soothe his ruptured ego. He had nothing – not even a way to take his laptop or books with him as he stepped across the threshold of his small house into a new dimension. With no more than the clothes on his back he stood at the end of the short driveway looking back toward the house at a car without gas, a house that was no longer a home and a career and life that he had enjoyed. Awaiting over his shoulder when he turned to face a new world was uncertainty, uncompromising doubt, and a savage world that expected money and credit cards. He had none of the essential tools for survival.

As evening fell, the southern California sun waned over the Hollywood hilltops in the west and the desert chill ensued. Hughes staggered more than walked in the direction of what shard of sunlight still existed, it seemed to be some sort of ray of hope. Perhaps in his mental oblivion he mistook it for a rainbow but regardless of what motivation he managed one foot in front of the next, and then the next, and so on as he moved toward central Pasadena from his eastside bungalow.

The loneliness of complete desperation provided Hughes with more than ample time to think and reflect on what had been and why it was no more. His time would have been better spent on the "how" for the future rather than the "why" for his ego but such was the condition of a man who had always felt superior to everyone else regardless of the absence of foundation.

Hughes was above begging like those at the ends of the freeway ramps who held small cardboard signs declaring war heroism and hard times or a houseful of kids and no job or spouse to help. He remembered how he had felt when he saw such desperate cases – they were to be looked down upon as inferior. Even now Hughes was unable to make the connection between such behavior and his own condition. Those people had brought their poverty and sadness upon themselves while he had been the target of an unjust system that had been solely motivated to get him. They, the bureaucrats, had had to cripple him in this fashion to bring him back to their level – to strike away his superiority and cause him to have to function in their world.

Eventually, Hughes without forethought, found himself behind some of the eating establishments along Colorado Boulevard scrounging through refuse bins for scraps of food and unfinished drinks – it had come to that. Retching up the remains of other peoples' discards had further fouled his clothes but such was of little concern to a man simply trying to remain alive.

At some point in his journey his weakened condition caused him to collapse – the cold exacting a further toll on his waning health. But then, the bright lights shone and the dream of academic accolades and scores of beautiful women fawning over him snapped away as shouting replaced the strains of chamber music that accompanied his dream.

"Get up!" shouted the jailer. "Get up, you bum!" He heard the threatening rebuke once again as he lay on a concrete floor amid a pool of urine and vomit. "What is it with you bums that you like to sleep in your own waste?" This time a laugh followed the rebuke, a scornful laugh. A clinking sound signaled the turning of a key in the lock of a large ironclad door. Instructions were shouted at Hughes who stood feebly as he and the cell were hosed down. Next the officer through in a towel and a simple but clean shirt and pair of pants. "Here! Get these on. You've got fifteen minutes and then we're throwing you out of here. Get a move on." The door slammed behind the large, square-shouldered officer whose blue uniform and badge told Hughes where he was, if not how he got there or why.

Hughes continued to tramp along in the same direction without reason or meaning. The gaunt former scholar left central Pasadena moving westward. As he did his passage took him across the old Colorado Street bridge better known as "Suicide Bridge." Pausing at the bridge's midpoint, Hughes looked down into the chasm, the Arroyo Seco, and thought about Brenda. She had done this to him. Thoughts of suicide crossed his mind, but he could not stomach the thought of the residual indignation. And he would never believe that the little tramp could have caused him this plight. His only recompense was the hope that continued to mount in his subconscious that her plight had ended up even worse than his own. Without a doubt she had been on a collision course with a drug overdose, a deadly case of HiV or simply throwing herself in front of an MTA bus to seek refuge from the miserable life she was caught within. Yes, his plight was her fault but satisfaction resided in the knowledge that she, without a doubt, was suffering much worse or was dead. *Screw that bitch. My qualities will be seen once again and my superior intellect will find my rewards. She'll not beat me.*

She's incapable of it. Hughes smirked as he turned his face away from the Arroyo Seco and continued to drag his tattered body across the span and on toward Glendale. . . and Hollywood.

The Flight of the Phoenix

Brenda's new career had taken off as surely as watching a plane rise off the runway. More critically, however, her life and her self-esteem were rising more like the fabled Phoenix from the ashes. Each day had become a new adventure with acting classes, voice lessons, discussions about current events all to round the personality and give depth to the property. Max Stern had agreed that his money would have been spent for naught if another "air head" hit the screen with a chest that out-weighed her brain. Max had a colorful way of putting this when speaking privately so as to avoid being misunderstood. And while the physical dimensions of her chest did in fact out-weight her brain the metaphor wasn't lost on either Brenda or her personal coach, Debbie.

Offers began to pour in by phone and by messenger to the little bungalow in the Hollywood Hills. Newsstand rags had all lined up to get a piece of the "new" star whose carefully coiffed and tailored look could grace any magazine but whose physical dimensions begged to be displayed on the popular T&A variety. Unbeknownst to such publishers,

photogs, and the phalanx of hucksters who spoke fast, leered and drooled as they made their pitch. While Brenda had reached a new plateau in understanding her new potential, it was Debbie who shut down such salacious offers that would get Brenda a few bucks and a return to the slide into oblivion. Debbie acted as "gatekeeper extraordinaire" in behalf of "the property" as Brenda had become known to those behind her new career. She was still "my sweetheart Brenda" to Debbie.

Likewise there was no shortage of men lining up without cameras in hand who wanted the new commodity. They, of course, loved Brenda and always had and now wanted to have the chance to spark the relationship and take Brenda out – harmlessly, of course, to dinner, to a Las Vegas show, an evening on the town. Debbie had been able to use Max Stern once again by invoking his name as the suitor who had gotten to the door first. The name was familiar to most but the turn-down was familiar to all; Debbie had once again provided the core of protection required to keep her friend on course, out of trouble and focused on her new life.

The classes and coaching had led Brenda to interviews and tryouts which, in turn, had given way to a contract, rehearsals, and eventually to filming. She had been chosen to star in a role that was essentially autobiographical. Neither Brenda nor Debbie had realized that Max had agreed to bankroll the film, seeking out other investors, finding a director and casting agent. Max had seen talent; he had seen the absence of talent and he saw in Brenda, potential. Her role could easily make her a star in tinsel town but the way she had arrived at the role and its fellowship with stardom would be legend and he had to be at the core of that success – not for Brenda, but for himself. His ego required it and his investment portfolio was seduced by it.

Filming had begun. Brenda had never been more focused or worked so hard in her life. In addition to the camera work there were interviews upon interviews. The first had been with the entertainment editor of the <u>Post</u> a couple months earlier when the project had been announced. The article had spawned a feeding frenzy by the media. The race had begun to see who could get the most onto paper or onto videotape first with the greatest in-depth synopsis of how this not-so-young girl had managed to overcome her upbringing, a stint with drugs and street-life tricks and then the overpowering impact of stereotyping resulting from her cresting in the porno industry.

The emphasis of the interviews was slowly changing. Max was quietly intervening from his high-rise office in Century City with magazine and newspaper editors. He had a fiduciary stake in the success of this project and this commodity, Brenda, and wanted to steer the conversation more toward her accomplishments, her talent, and her potential than to dwell on the sins of the past. It was working.

The dailies are the day's production of film that is reviewed by the director and others. This day's review had given rise to exhilaration and to a procedure that had begun arduously and cautiously. The mood and tempo had increased, and the air about the set had become electric as the cast and crew watched the young / not-so-young woman, age unknown, move through her lines with grace and ease. The role was a natural for Brenda – her greatest difficulty was to treat this strictly as a job and not a slice of her actual life. A couple earlier lapses into memory had ended in tears and a collapse. She was past that now and rolling like a juggernaut demonstrating in each scene that she had always been meant to be here, in this role, in this life and with her close friend Debbie.

149

Frogtown

The trek continued and had become a painful, resolute endeavor the aim of which had never become fixed in the head of Malcolm Hughes. An attraction, a magnet, destiny had pulled him along Colorado Boulevard and now into the city of Glendale where the street had changed names to Broadway. Still, nomenclature notwithstanding, he moved from the rear of one McDonald's to another from one respite to another trying to avoid the teenage gangs who liked to beat transients to death, trying to avoid starving to death, and trying to avoid incarceration once again.

Friday night: he had gotten as far as the east side of Glendale stumbling along without cause. Bright lights illuminated the sky ahead of him; from time to time, cheering erupted in some spasmodic display of appreciation. It was a football game Hughes concluded as he found a few untapped neurons not dedicated solely to the purpose of self-preservation. As he passed the stadium the bright lights and cheering continued; a sign read "Loyola 52 – Mater Dei 0."

The significance meant nothing. The score didn't feed him or clothe him and he could think of no way to use it against Brenda.

Hughes moved through the shadowy night from store front to store front and from refuse bin to refuse bin. He had found a dollar bill along the curb in the eastside of town and parlayed it into a cup of McDonald's coffee. While watched closely by the management he finally took a seat on the far side of the child-friendly fast food establishment at a table where some irresponsible patrons had not bothered to dispose of their own trash. Hughes' dulled wit managed a quiet eureka! He quickly slid into the booth ate the balance of the fries and a remaining nugget. As the manager came toward him embracing a scowl that could be felt as well as seen, Hughes abruptly cut his dining experience short and exited back to the street and continued his westward trek.

The line of march brought the now-vagrant to the Los Angeles River – famed for being a concrete chasm without water. This was late-Fall and there were only a few pools and a small stream that ran through a culvert within the concrete river bed. He had arrived at a decent place to spend the night. He identified an area where no gang thugs could sneak up on him. There were small patches of brush that had sprung to live and flourished from a single crack between concrete slabs. Here would be a place to spend the night before chancing his way over the culvert and across the abutting freeway. The mere thought of the name of the freeway brought a shudder to Hughes body: the Golden State Freeway. Golden equals gold, gold equals money, money equals food, a place to live and some clothes to wear. Hughes' brain was beginning a disconnect process. The Golden State motto reflected the pre-eminent color to be seen in one vista after another due to the type of ground cover within the generally desert climate and the fact that it turned a golden color except during the brief rainy period in the loosely defined period called, *winter*.

Hughes settled into a clump of reeds and grasses using a piece of cardboard as a mattress. He curled into the fetal position to retain as much body heat as possible during the chilly night. Sleep. He needed sleep and strength to go on. This would be an uncommonly ignominious end to a celebrated life as Hughes saw it. It couldn't end here. He would battle on – to what end he had no idea.

As the witching hour of the night crept in so did an all too familiar sound for this area about which Hughes was unaware - the sound of frogs and toads croaking throughout the night. An endless rhythm of squawks and squeaks eventually became as ear-splitting as a front row rock concert seat.

He moved on.

Scaling a chain link fence Hughes weakened condition was barely enough to enable him to dart between the all too frequent eighty mile per hour vehicles that roared along the GSF or I-5 Freeway. Terrified at several close calls from Death's Angel, Hughes scaled the fence on the opposing side of the roadway as he entered the perimeter of Griffith Park and the adjacent Gene Autry Museum parking lot. The park would afford a great many more places to huddle for the balance of the night but the number of critters in this huge natural environment would keep him awake until dawn broke over the eastern horizon.

Chilled to the bone, the question that had followed behind him on his trek of nearly a week had finally caught up to him and now rested with him like a silent companion. He needed to address this companion because surely the

companion had every intention of addressing him. The companion's name was "death." Did he want to meet this companion and follow him wherever he might lead or garner some more strength to fight on? The decision was overpowering and just the process of having to negotiate a response to his subconscious he rose from the ground and shouted "damn you Brenda! I'll kill you, you bitch."

Hughes began his hike around the perimeter of the park and into the Los Feliz district of Los Angeles. *I'm not dead yet*, he thought.

In the Can

The tedium had lasted for months: lessons, interviews, the constant exposure to higher culture, body wraps, rehearsals, and more lessons. The pace did not slow once Brenda had been selected to star in the film "Queen." Quite the contrary, now the eye of the camera was on her constantly and the metamorphosis that had been developed to consume the "old" Brenda had to demonstrate that there was substance beneath the glossy exterior, not just a shallow image upon which the "twins" were hung so adoringly.

Interviews and requests for photos shoots from the conventional men's magazines, the T&A variety, gave way to Penthouse, then to Playboy. All such requests were summarily rejected by Debbie, the consummate overseer. Slowly the requests began to emerge from People, Us, Cosmo and that ilk – general societal readership exposure and each was granted. Brenda was becoming a real person, a part of society and not recognized simply for what she had been but for what she had become and what she could yet be.

The fringe benefits had a spill-over effect in that Debbie, acting as agent, was also exposed to the same people and opportunities. But like the "power behind the throne" Debbie remained true to her role of gatekeeper and agent-extraordinaire. She shunned any limelight and deferred to Brenda pushing her image and career constantly.

Over the months since Debbie had bamboozled Max Stern into underwriting the costs and use of his network to gain the required exposure thoughts about the true genesis of this turn of events had become lost. Debbie recalled sex with Max Stern as the turning point in the chain of events. She remembered with particular emphasis as her interests in men had been depleted after years of sex the hard way in alleys, the front seats of cars, and cheap hotels. Her friendship with Brenda had gradually morphed into a close friendship and eventually love.

Brenda's recollections had become skewed by the change in every aspect of her life that had been required. So many lessons, so many interviews, so much coaching, so much reading of current events and novels "of substance" had shortened her memory.

All the preparation had reached its peak. The filming of "Queen" had culminated and was "in the can" as Hollywood producers and directors are given to say. Oh sure, the interviews continued, in fact, the number increased as it became clear that the picture had substance as a serious piece of work, but the pressure was now released into the atmosphere. Brenda, and Debbie, could let forth with a sigh of relief. They had done it. If the film was taken seriously and made some money new offers would roll in for the new star. . . and her agent. A whole new career could unveil itself to each of them. With Hollywood, it was all about dollars. If the film made money, it was successful. In the remainder of

the world beyond Hollywood and Vine the measure was a little more abstract: could the moviegoers relate to the character? Was she a beautiful new star? Was she an "air head" or could she walk and talk at the same time? Would people go back and see her in another film – the true test of stardom. Those questions loomed in the minds of both Brenda and Debbie but they also loomed in the mind of the financially-committed Max Stern, his fellow backers, the studio, and a host of technicians who made their living off the success of such people as Brenda. Time would tell and that time was rapidly approaching. The premier of the movie had been set for Saturday evening, just a few days away.

Over the preceding weekend Brenda and Debbie had joyfully sat atop a stack of pillows on the deck that overhung one of the canyons in the Hollywood Hills. They scanned all the magazines and newspapers like little kids gleefully bouncing about with new toys. The chatter was about what the critics were saying; it was about the results of various interviews that had been given and it was about a new life. "Oh Debbie. . . I have you to thank for this." Before Debbie could downplay her role Brenda continued adjusting her mood from one of giddiness to sincerity. "I am completely aware of everything you have done for me including your intercession with Max Stern. I know what you did for him to deflect him from me and keep him at bay until he changed directions. All the finagling and negotiations and arrangements. . . you have done it all. I know and I am grateful beyond words. And what is most important is I know why you did it. . . and yes, I love you too."

Horrors
and Scores of Whores

And still he rambled on. . . .

Hughes, looking increasingly haggard and desperate, sustained himself on things most people would never eat, but then most people were not caught in his dilemma. His sole motivation was to continue to move toward some unknown goal in the hope of discovering that motivating force and once again provide purpose and sustenance to his life.

Circumventing the perimeter of the largest metropolitan park in the U.S., Hughes staggered his way down Los Feliz Street the next day– Los Feliz was a street wholly unknown to him but it was more or less straight ahead so he trudged on. He had traversed only about twelve or thirteen miles but it had taken him a week to move this far. Los Feliz jogged to the left; Hughes jogged to the left. Mid-afternoon and already the hookers were there. He had arrived at Hollywood Boulevard, "The" Boulevard as that stupid bitch Brenda had identified it.

Christ. Was this it? Was this the unseen force that had pulled him unconsciously through a week's unending pain and hunger? Had the god of wrath and vengeance circled his life back to Hollywood so he could encounter Brenda? Screw the god of wrath and vengeance. I would no sooner let Brenda see me in this condition than I'd be willing to meet with Steingrit in the men's room in a municipal park. Perhaps, based on the findings of my study I can find a way to parlay that in some beneficial way to turn my fortunes around. A good place to start would be the Hollywood Star or the Hollywood Reporter. Those "rags" would love to buy what I have to say about the little tart. Then with the money I'll eat, get some clothes and then pay a visit to Brenda and that dyke friend of hers. Perhaps I'll buy a gun before I show up at her place and fix her life like she's fixed mine. It would be only fair. Hughes's mind rambled from one thought to another without direction but a new sense of purpose had finally been kindled within him, a motivation that had been lacking since the USC dismissal and especially since being thrown out of his house and onto the street. *Yes, I have a purpose now, and Brenda is once again at the heart of it. Yes, I can see it now. I'll get a gun and force her to perform a few of her famous tricks on me while she pleads for her life and then when she's done, she's done. . . for good.*

Hughes began the last of his sojourn across Hollywood, the east end of the community-within-the-city of Los Angeles. He had heard about street hookers from Brenda, he had read about them in the Times and on the television news, but he had never had to work his way through them like a gauntlet. In the east end of Hollywood they were a dime a dozen, the crack whores, the young kids who'd run away from home like Brenda to get away or to make an easy fortune in the movies. They all had ended up in the same sewer living like rats in a tenement, eating scantily, doing drugs of every

variety and price and scoring one trick after another to pay "the man." *Was this what Brenda had been? If so, she did well to pull herself out of this swamp and onto something akin to dry ground. Brenda was bad, she was at the bottom of the food chain but these kids, these haggard-looking women wearing outfits that barely covered the critical parts of their bodies, these women whose bodies carried one disease or another and had track marks up and down the arms and legs weren't even in the food chain to stretch the analogy. Damn, it's worse than I realized.*

"No. No! Get out of here, leave me alone." Hughes rejected one insipid offer for sex after another. Each new offer making him feel more like a man that women were throwing themselves at him. Hughes's mind was caught once again between ego and reason. He was disgusted by what he saw and the pathetic excuse for a life that was cast before him one doorway after another. Yet each offer further aroused him. The greatest irony of all was that Hughes in his degenerated condition was a far greater mess than any of the abused souls trying to score a trick for drug money. Obviously the street whores were no more desperate than Hughes but the ego-infused Hughes was incapable of understanding any of this.

Ahead. Keep going. Left. Right. Keep Going. His feet, bare within his dilapidated shoes, were black and punctuated with red-festered sores. His torso was hunched and hung with filthy and self-stained remnants of what remained of his jail-provided wardrobe. His bony hands, like his feet, were darkened from his constant exposure to the outside and were sticky with the residue of food scraps found in refuse receptacles. Hughes's face was the telltale indicator of the outcome of falsifying a report to the federal government. His hair was matted and grungy; the splotchy beard patches were positively disgusting to view. His eyes,

however, were the ultimate sign of despair. Sunken, dark and seemingly without signs of life behind them, his eyes indicated he was already dead. The rest of his body simply hadn't as yet gotten the same message.

He had moved along far enough now that the sense of social orientation of "The Boulevard" had changed. The crack whores, the gang members sitting atop their cars challenging everyone to pass through "their hood" had given way to local business types and tourists.

Ahead Hughes could see a building with a sign: "Hollywood Reporter." *At last*, he thought, *I've made it.*

Metro Transit Authority

Getting past the lobby guard had been a challenge but eventually he ended up sitting across from a disheveled young man who pecked away at his keyboard as Hughes spoke. Malcolm Hughes, Ph.D., had shown his university ID from his wallet and made the claim that his appearance was part of an experiment about which he was conducting research and writing a paper for the university. The logic had seemed reasonable to the young man who, while keeping his eyes trained elsewhere, allowed Hughes to walk his way through his story about Brenda.

When the two were complete, Hughes asked for payment in cash rather than a voucher or check indicating the obvious that in his disguise he'd not be able to cash a check.

Two doors further to the west Hughes came to appreciate why so many are killed in our society with handguns as he was able to purchase a gun and cartridges despite his appearance. A few doors further he found McDonalds. By the time he had finished stuffing himself he had overcompensated for his hunger and began vomiting as

soon as he had gagged his way out of the restaurant and to the curb.

As his faculties began to return he realized that he had just destroyed the paint job on a new Corvette but that was of little concern to him. His attention had been pulled across the street and down a block. A din of noise rose and fell several times, the rotating spectacle of a truck-drawn set of spotlights gave focus to some sort of human circus taking place just ahead.

Hughes had his mission now. His agenda was fixed, however, the curiosity of the event before him tugged at his feet as surely as at his mind. He staggered forward and there it was – a movie marquee. In breathtakingly large letters it said, "QUEEN," starring Brenda.

A sense of rage swept over Hughes much the same way that a tornado sweeps over a small town and its inevitable mobile homes. A froth formed at the corners of Hughes's lips, his eyes took on a fixation and his body had become taut, his stringy muscles drawn up tightly.

There she is. Goddamn her, there she is. I'd recognize that bitch anywhere with her "celebrated twins." This is perfect. She has come to me as a self-sacrifice for all the pain and suffering she has caused me. Her guilt has just been announced publicly in massive lettering on a signboard high enough for everyone to read. The marquee didn't say "QUEEN" starring Brenda. Hughes re-read the sign and there it was: I'm at fault. I caused all your problems. I am guilty and I have come here tonight to accept your wrath and your payback. Shoot me!"

Brenda stood on the sidewalk among hundreds of screaming fans, tourists and the merely curious. Screams and shouts for autographs punctuated the deafening din emanating from the massive crowd. She stood at the street end of a red carpet that had been drawn between her now-departed limousine and the front door to Grauman's Chinese Theater where the premier of her movie was being shown. Brenda was draped in an elegant evening dress, red sequined, plunging neckline to allow the "twins" their day at the premier, and perfectly form-fitting. She rotated from side to side waving to the well-wishers, smiling a becoming smile and holding the hand of another woman.

Hughes began crossing the street directly toward Brenda. His body fell forward with each step as he staggered toward the goal that had pulled him along on this journey. He reached into his pocket, withdrew the revolver, and pointed it toward Brenda. Some of the cheering crowd saw the event unfolding and began to scream and disperse; Brenda rolled her body toward the crazy, delusional man inching his way forward toward her with a gun aimed in her direction.

Hughes moved as if being drawn across a guide track. His eyes were completely focused on his target and the salvation his soul sought for the misery this woman had brought down upon him. He was now thirty feet away and close enough to begin firing. He would empty all the chambers into her body and say thank you for each as it struck her. His eyes seemed to turn red like those of a hunting animal as he pulled back the hammer.

THUD! Screeeeeech! Squisiiish, Screams enveloped the crowd. Some were running away, some running toward and some just running amok. Brenda stood in place, frozen in time. Her hand rose instinctively to cover her mouth as she gasped at the sight to which she had just been witness. Some crazy man had just been struck full force by an MTA bus and crushed beneath its wheels.

The police officers on duty for crowd control immediately took charge of the scene. They made every effort to get people away from the bus and refocused on the premier as a way to reduce the investigation of the accident.

The producers and theater officials immediately jumped into action to refocus the crowd and pump new life into the excitement of the premier and downplay what had just taken place.

Brenda was stunned but her future pulled her along the red carpet.

Debbie, who seldom missed a cue, had recognized Hughes. She tucked her arm into that of Brenda's and whispered, "that crazy guy was most likely some religious fanatic, the kind who carry signs about the end of the earth and all. Most likely he objected to your movie because of your earlier life. Don't worry about it baby. This man was destined for this end."

Epilog

QUEEN had been a success, an overwhelming success in fact. The premier had jolted the movie to the top of the lists and then the curious and those drawn by the peculiar events surrounding the premier and that poor man under the wheels of the bus bolstered the revenue stream beyond anyone's wildest dreams.

Max Stern had succeeded in playing the odds and his investment had reaped profits far in excess of his revenues from his more conventional clients. The studios were thrilled and immediately signed Brenda to a multi-film deal worth zillions of dollars.

Brenda had become wealthy beyond reason immediately and her liaison, Debbie, had also drawn down from the excesses of public curiosity. Talk of awards began to flourish almost immediately.

Coming from a broken home life with an abusing father, a stint with drugs and street life and even a career as a porno queen would be devastating for someone trying to become a success in the business world. However, in Hollywood such is not the case – it's called the development of character and depth.

Sundays were still spent as before with the two girls in their "jammies" reading the columns on politics and current events as well as the funny papers. They were truly a twosome now and happy in their new place. The small bungalow in the Hollywood Hills had given rise to a very large place in another of the "hills" communities, Beverly Hills.

A couple days after the premier of QUEEN Debbie had gone to the Office of the County Coroner and made arrangements for the burial of Hughes. She slipped out of their little place before Brenda had risen so as to keep any pain from her friend. Even this jerk, Debbie thought, deserved to be properly buried.

Unbeknownst to Debbie, every year thereafter, Brenda made her way to that grave site and said a short prayer and apologized.

Oh, and by the way. Dennis was given full authority for teaching all of Hughes's classes as he was eminently better qualified than his mentor. For his part, Dennis took the new role to heart. Actually, he took it to his ear, his nose, his tongue and his penis with a series of piercings. After all, this was a class in Psychology, right?

About the Author

If there has to be a *light side* to anything. Jerry will find it. Analytically, this aspect of his character kept him in the Vice Principal's office or the Dean's List in near perpetuity but has now found a meaningful outlet.

Brenda and two successive novels, Ruthie and Vivian are a quantum takeoff from his normal writing interests which tend toward intrigue and mayhem – spies and war.

www.ingramcontent.com/pod-product-compliance
Lightning Source LLC
Chambersburg PA
CBHW071248130626
46556CB00003B/1218